Crazigasm

JK Hirani

First published in 2017 by

Becomeshakespeare.com
Wordit Content Design & Editing Services Pvt Ltd
Unit - 26, Building A-1, Nr Wadala RTO, Wadala (East),
Mumbai 400037, India
T:+91 8080226699

This book has been fully funded by the Wordit Art Fund.
Wordit Art Fund helps deserving authors publish their work by
providing monetary support. To apply for funding, please visit us at
www.BecomeShakespeare.com

©
ISBN: 978-93-86487-26-1

DEDICATION

To my fast and furious wife who brings balance to my life, who has never watched the TV series Friends but is the replica of Monica, a neat-freak and highly competitive woman. Love you Kavya and your dal fry.

CRAZIGASM

ACKNOWLEDGMENTS

Nothing on this planet can be done alone. Even feeding a food to someone involves roughly 180 hands right from land cultivation to food preparation. Same way, this book too would not have been possible without the efforts of few people and many others who inadvertently contributed to its making.

This book like every other book is an amalgamation of thoughts from various people and their situations. The picture created in a writer's subconscious mind is later on printed on paper. I strongly believe that God chooses His people to do a certain task. I thank Him that He chose me to unveil this story in front of you.

My parents, for being there. Always. No matter what.

My joint family, for giving me the emotions and thereby helping me to express myself.

Ashok Jha, for being the definition of friendship which includes a blindfold trust.

Pradeep Mohanani, for being a 4am friend and introducing me to an amazing foods of the world thereby making me realize that if there is a good food on the table, life is lovely.

Ankit Arora, for showing me a path less travelled, only travelled by the dreamers.

Nishit Shah, for giving me a tough time by being a harsh critic, very harsh. Extremely harsh.

Yashwant Chobisa, for humor, period.

My brother, Yogesh Lakshman, for designing a beautiful cover for this book.

Mahan Team of construction engineers, for germinating the seed of author in me and giving me all the beautiful memories to cherish for lifetime.

Microsoft, for without it, editing would have been a herculean task.

Google, for making me intelligent every day and helping me research anything, anytime.

Seva Café, for connecting the disconnected souls through food.

Madhu and Meghna, for making me realize the importance and power of meditation.

Vaibhav Himthani, a child prodigy whose energy and passion in life is a great motivating factor for me.

Shiva Dubey, a delhite bc, who taught me that there is always a time for some fun.

Musicians, lyricists and singers, for when nothing works out in life, I go straight to them and then suddenly like a miracle, everything starts working again.

There are many others and the list is endless but this acknowledgement section cannot be done without mentioning her name. She is my beautiful, charming vivacious and endearing wife, Kavya Hirani. With her unstinted support, her heart of gold and her will of diamond, anything comes within limit in this limitless world.

A heartfelt thanks to all the people mentioned here and my well-wishers across the globe.

CRAZIGASM

1

National highway no. 8 must have felt fortunate when those two sexy legs fell on it. They carried a shapely figure with a waving hand and the tresses fell on that beautiful face. The widespread mountains of Aravali range also felt amorphous after watching her curves. The Sun augmented her beauty with the sunlight. She resembled a cloudy sky in her white top and denim shorts. When she was gathering the attention of the whole nature, the poor truck driver was bound to stop at her waving hand.

The Altaf Raja hit of 90's *'Tum to thehre pardesi'* was playing on the radio. The crack on the windshield was evident. A lungi and a kurta were hanging on a hook behind the driver's seat. A big head below the turban, two kilo beard and a distended belly above the lungi were clearly visible of that driver. With a mild hangover post heavy lunch and a few pegs of country liquor, he tried to maintain his focus on that lonely road. While driving a transportation truck every day, beautiful roads don't amaze you much, nor the natural beauty. But this enchanting creation of the Almighty trying to stop the truck ballooned his half opened eyes to witness something ethereal on a barrenly boring highway.

He jumped off the truck grinning, and shut the door with his heavy hand showing his excitement.

"Oye pari kithe chali?" (Oh angel, where are you going?), he asked in his local heavy accent.

The angel fidgeted out of nervousness.

"What happened? Where do you want to go?" the driver asked her again while she tried to locate someone on a deserted highway.

"Are you deaf?" he kept probing her, to which she smiled and shook her head.

"Ok," he said scratching his beard. "Are you mute?" he asked again thinking quickly.

"Huh" she sighed and thought, "*Where are you Rishabh?*"

"Oh God," he said disgruntled, looking towards the sky, "Such a beautiful girl and you forgot to give her a voice. How uncreative of you?"

While driver was busy complaining to God, the dilapidated engine of the truck cried to life but he was so lost in her beauty that he couldn't hear anything except her mute and cute expressions. She fiercely signaled towards the moving truck but the enchanted driver refused to look away.

"Oye madam," he said, dejected, "I know that you want to go with me in this truck but let me first have a word with God for not providing you the voice."

"Your truck is moving Dumbo," her sudden sweet and commanding voice terminated his grievance session with God.

He instantly switched his glances between the truck and the girl and then went into the traumatic dilemma of which shock to handle first, a moving truck or the moving lips. Finally he ran after his truck leaving behind the angel who could speak by now.

The angel quickly ran towards the other lane of the highway while the truck stopped at a distance, the driver still running behind it. From the left hand door of the truck came down a manly figure in a flash of a second and he also ran towards the other lane but his reflexes are too fast to notice him. Let's observe him in a slow motion.

From the left door of the truck, came down an athletic figure in a white shirt and the blue denims. His shirt gripped his nicely carved out muscles. The stubble on his chiseled face and a layered messy hairstyle complemented his virile structure. He jumped off the truck in a parkour style, his khaki sport shoes supporting him. He crossed the divider in one leap and reached near his glossy black Yamaha R1 where the angel was already waiting for him.

The driver reached near his truck and realized that he has been mocked by the couple. The buttery smooth highways are always filled with hindrances. Dealing with goons and thieves on roads is normal for these drivers so they always carry some kind of a weapon along with them. He took out a steel pipe from underneath his seat and ran after them. The beautiful couple in white and blue on black R1 disappeared in no time.

The plush R1 moving at a speed of 190 Km/hr carrying a dashing couple on a national highway amongst the mountains looked surreal and perfect. Even the Hindu mythological Gods above the clouds savored the scene.

"Poor driver," said Rishabh, the biker, placing two cups of coffee on a table at "Baba da Dhaba" a roadside restaurant in the suburbs of Abu road.

"No sympathies please, did you see how he was looking

at me when he got down?" retorted Angel (yes her name is Angel).

"Not his fault. Your eyegasmic looks cause hypnosis. If looks could heal there would be no doctors in this world, only your videos in every hospital."

"You never get tired of flirting, do you?" she asked, her amatory adventure on a romantic journey with him adding one more curve to her body with a smile.

"Tired of flirting with the lady with surprises? No, I don't," he answered and took a sip of coffee in a chilly weather of just begun December.

"Well, I like to get bigger surprises from you by giving you the smaller ones," she said looking sensuously into his eyes without blinking hers.

Without worrying about the number of eyes watching them both, Rishabh's eyes were locked into Angel's and then he leaned forward to lock his lips into hers. The caffeine flavored kiss came to a halt when Angel's phone rang.

"Its mom," she exclaimed, after taking out her phone from her shorts.

"Fuck! How will you handle her now?"

"Don't steal my statement. Take this phone," she immediately shot, handing over the phone and making herself more comfortable on a chair, sipping coffee.

"Ruthless," Rishabh murmured.

"Thank you. Now pick up the phone and turn on the speaker. I like it when she scolds you."

Even before Rishabh could greet her, the lady on the other side had already started.

"What on the earth are you doing at Baba da Dhaba?" the authoritarian asked.

Rishabh's eyes started scanning around for a spy after his nervous system sent the signal to his brain with a tag of *shocking* on it.

"How on the earth do you know that mom?" he asked after a lot of processing by his brain.

"Oh, so she gave the phone to you. Are you both crazy, going to Mt. Abu from Ahmedabad on a bike without your jackets on? And you said you were going for a movie and now you are in Abu. Why can't you both just sit at home? It's been two years since your marriage and you still behave like kids."

They both listened to the speaker of the phone like kids, still perplexed how their location was revealed to the mother.

"Now say something," mom said angrily.

"Baba da Dhaba, how did you know that?" Rishabh enquired with eyes and mouth open wide, Angel's too.

"My dear son, don't try to outsmart the lady who kept you in her womb for nine months. I turned on the geo tagging in your phones before you left."

They both looked at each other in amazement and then Rishabh asked, "Since when you started using smart phones mom?"

"Well, your silly wife taught me once. Now bring back my daughter-in-law safely. Poor girl trapped with my stupid son."

"Poor girl?" Rishabh asked in question. "It was all her idea to have a coffee in Abu and ride back home without warm clothes on in the evening."

"No mom it was Rishabh who drove me here," Angel spoke for the first time on phone.

"Liar," Rishabh said. "You only told me outside that

multiplex that Mt. Abu is such a nice place.

"Yes, but then you started the bike and took me here."

"Well you did not resist me also."

"I am a pativrata (virtuous) woman. How can I go beyond my husband's will?"

Mom interrupted in between, "Stop fighting you both. Kidults. Just come back home now."

"Ok mom," they both said in unison.

"And yes. Buy some cookies from that dhaba. Your Dad loves it."

"When did you and dad come here?" Angel asked smiling with Rishabh.

"What do you think? You are the only crazy couple out there. The only difference is, your dad and I went on Bajaj scooter instead of R1. Now come back and drive safely. I am waiting."

"Ok mom," Rishabh disconnected the call.

"I love her" Angel beamed.

Rishabh caressed her hand, kissed it and went on to buy cookies.

"Why did you want to stop that truck?" he asked while starting the bike.

"I just wanted to copy those actresses in movies who stop vehicles by showing their legs. I wanted to see whether it really works. But why didn't you ask me the reason about it then. You just said *Go Ahead*."

"Because patnivrata pati I am," he said.

She hugged him tighter and rested her head on his shoulder.

R1 gained some acceleration on a creamy wide national highway. The bike's speed and the Angel's embrace gave an adrenaline ride to Rishabh making him feel to go fast and slow at the same time, fast on bike speed and slow on life. The delicate rubbing of Angel's cheek with his and her intermittent kisses on his neck gave ticklish chill with some more adrenalin gust inside him.

"Are you cold?" he asked after some time.

"Fucking freezing," she moaned.

"Then use your heater."

"Alright," she said and Rishabh felt her hands slowly travelling from his shoulders. They moved to his torso giving him mini shocks like defibrillator. His thighs moved a little closer to the petrol tank with her ultra-sensitive touch and then those naughty hands lastly landed onto his groin, the final destination to begin the scientific process of heat conduction.

Even the Sun took some time before hiding in the Aravali range to catch few more glimpses of that amorous couple in deep love.

2

"I have never been so high," Viren said gulping neat whiskey.

"Height or booze?" Rishabh asked looking down from a seven storey high concrete water tank constructed near airport, sitting on the edge of its boundary.

"Height of course. This fucking whiskey alone never takes me high. "Yes but," he swigged another sip, "when Shyna pours me something," he had a hiccup, "anything, even water, it takes me high enough that I never want to come down anytime soon. Her deep glistening eyes looking at me sensuously, her perfectly manicured hands pouring whiskey for me, her seductive voice deluding me from the pangs of harsh life, only a pathetically ridiculous freak would want to remain low in front of that sex goddess whose perfectly pristine orgasms would make me believe that being with her is the sole purpose of my life."

Rishabh looked at Viren with a twisted eye. "Wow, are you wearing my shoes today?" he jibed watching his shoes, taking up his hanging legs.

"Oh no. I can never write like you. You are one hell of a writer. You have this ability to stimulate every individual's mental clitoris and create a storm of emotions inside. I am a born ten per center. I was never creative. I get my orgasmic feeling when I sell the work of highly talented people like you to the best of the best buyers in the country whatever it takes, blow jobs included."

Even the shoddy words of Viren could not bring smile on Rishabh's face. The pain was far too fierce to be subjugated by anything. Even jumping off from the height would not have numbed the pain. In fact the thought of death would have only increased the pain further because it would have been selfish to escape through death and putting Angel alone in trauma.

The pain of separation from Angel was no less than that of Karna while cutting his armor and earrings in Mahabharata. Rishabh was shattered to the core. Feeling vulnerable he found shelter in Viren's hug.

"Thank you for being here." Rishabh expressed gratitude under a stormy dark night in a cracking voice. "Before any giant agent you are my brother."

Viren was totally aware of his emotional wreckage and he knew the only way to alleviate his pain was to make him speak more.

"How did we land up ourselves in this shit?" he asked Rishabh pouring him some whiskey. "You two were invincible. What and where it all went wrong in this perfect love story?"

"I have no fucking idea what went wrong. I was busy admiring so much of rightness in our relationship that the wrong was an uncalled guest," Rishabh said in a gloomy voice looking into the darkness taking another sip. "Her esurience for craziness is the best gift I have ever received in my life. She came like a typhoon which I never wanted to slow down. She is the living example of creating abundance. Even the tiniest thought of her amplifies my emotions, you can imagine what must be happening when she is around. My body and soul get in sync whenever I am with her. She is my topmost priority deserving highest maintenance."

The sober and clear words of Rishabh, even after intake of whiskey, penetrated Viren's ears making him realize that pain is only going to aggravate on tomorrow's disastrous day but he let Rishabh speak. Consoling and making him quiet would have only worsened the situation.

"She is a total freak," Rishabh could not stop remembering the moments with her. "You know we would go into a random college and she would deliver a lecture on a sex education in a random class while I would patrol outside making weird excuses to professors to not let them in. We even distributed condoms in college campuses on several occasions. She used to go on a construction site and do some work along with female laborers thereby encouraging and motivating them. She would wear a white sari with a candle in her hand and wake up the sleeping security guard on duty."

"And you were the lucky motherfucker to savor all the flavors of her craziness," Viren said opening another bottle and pouring in the glass.

"True that. I am a gold medalist from Luck University." A writer with a wounded soul is always lethal with words. "The memories of our first meeting are still invigorating like a mountain air. That day I could not satiate myself with enough of her playfulness."

Rishabh's musings about Angel kept him afloat in that

dark night of sorrows.

3

The eye catching personality of Rishabh in a black Prada blazer was hard to miss. Playful wavy hair, black shirt, dark blue denims, light black woodland shoes, he was a synonym for class. Walking outside his house, he put on the Carrera aviator sun glasses with a metal frame over his light colored eyes. His hand wearing Tag Heuer wristwatch with black leather strap opened the door of his convertible Porsche. He grabbed the steering and turned on the ignition. The glossy metallic black Porsche roared in a most decent manner and moved elegantly escaping the pot holes. The melodious sound of engine could not continue much as there was a traffic jam ahead.

While most of them in the jam were cribbing and cursing as they were getting late for their nine-to-five hatefully loved jobs where they practice adulatory in front and spitefulness at the back, Rishabh was at ease. It was his observation time. Every morning he used to take a ride in the town and just observe people with their situations, a rider writer on hunt for some beautiful lines. After all, a writer can only be as good as his observations.

He used five years of his spare time sacrificing the most

important frivolous activities of bickering, FBing, Whatssaping, practicing idleness during his job days and built a solid pipeline of income which could never cease to give outflow of money even if Rishabh was sick, out on vacation or not working at all. Two of his title works had already hit the silver screen and generated tremendous business. Whenever he had to deliver a speech somewhere, he would motivate people to use 5 years of spare time in creativity to save 50 years of full time in mediocrity.

Traffic jams for us, the democratic Indians is just another medium to vent out the frustration on our Government but we don't realize that mostly these jams are because of our ill driving etiquettes rather than the inefficiency of the Government. It's like blaming a condom brand for pregnancy while in reality we don't know its proper usage. And Amdawadi (native of Ahmedabad) drivers are renowned for the misuse. They don't realize that excitement of haste is ephemeral while the real pleasure is in slow movements and I was of course talking about driving here with an intended pun.

One such hasty prick hit a cow and ran away. The cow lay injured in the middle of the road resulting in a traffic jam.

As soon as Rishabh passed nearby the accident spot in that slow moving traffic, he parked his car at some distance and quickly jumped out to help the creature.

He started running towards the pain ridden cow but the moment his sight fell on a turquoise Punjabi suit with something fetching inside it, his running became bovine, cacophony of vehicles seemed melodious and the smoke from autos looked like theatrical fog.

Her animated hand moved in desperation, her 1.618

golden ratio face looked little tensed but it reflected the same positive energy as dew drops on leaf. Her straight loosened hair enjoyed the freedom of playing with the wind while she periodically tried to stop them from overplaying. The silver bindi (decoration) on her forehead was like some artist's days of hard work to give a finishing touch to his art. Rishabh saw her large American almond shaped black glistening eyes from distance and found himself to be lost in there for a while. In his reverie, she said something with her fuller lips in ultra-slow motion over the phone. She looked like a definition of perfection.

"How is she?" Rishabh asked reaching the spot trying to maintain his semblance.

"In severe pain. Asshole hit the pregnant lady," she said. Her silvery voice augmented her beauty. Rishabh noticed the bulge of the cow in a microsecond and quickly focused back on her. Taking his eyes off her was like carrying a huge log of wood. It was a lot of hard work.

"Thanks for stopping by," she continued mesmerizing him with her voice, with her looks, with her expressions, with her smell, with her concern for a cow. "Everybody seems to be robotic here. Humanity is dying exponentially," she said, furiously trying to call someone. "And my battery too. Plus this rescue center is useless. Nobody is picking up the phone."

"Don't worry. I got a Vet's number. Good friend," Rishabh said and called one of his contacts, his brain now functioning faster than the usual.

Within minutes the rescue team arrived, gave an emergency treatment to a mother and took her with them for further medical care.

"You want me to drop you somewhere?" Rishabh asked her.

"Oh yes of course. Where is your chariot?"

"Over there," Rishabh pointed towards Porsche.

"Run, run, run," she accelerated Rishabh.

They jumped inside the car and fastened the seat belts. Before Rishabh could say a word, she fired, "Listen. Before you turn on your beauty, here are few instructions. I need to be at an event in Courtyard Marriot in next fifteen minutes which means you will have to show your best performance in driving without actually driving fast but you can't drive slow also, so Mr. equilibrist, I know that I am beautiful and you would want to impress me but this car of yours is not a slouch either, please don't hurt her. What's your name by the way?"

"Rishabh and you are?"

"Terribly late for an event"

"Keep talking Miss-Terribly-late-for-an-event. I have started liking this feeling of being in some alien world," Rishabh said as he gracefully rolled the wheels, coming out of his slow motion reverie to a fast paced adventurous ride.

They just crossed a kilometer and there was another traffic jam. The Porsche stopped later, the lady jumped out of it prior in a Singham (Bollywood movie) style. She climbed up the bonnet of the Porsche and started giving signals to clear the traffic. Nobody could ignore the enchanting diva, they all were yielding to her instructions like Rishabh and traffic got cleared. She jumped back in and the engine roared again. She was a riot, a never ending roller coaster ride.

Watching Rishabh drive so smoothly she asked

inquisitively, "What are you? A transporter or something, like Jason Statham (Hollywood actor), looking highly polished, driving a German car, being laconic. Am I going to be in a deep shit being with you right now? Do you have guns inside you? Can you perform those fight moves like Jason?"

Rishabh was just smiling and enjoying her euphonious chattering while she kept her vocal chords at work.

"You must be thinking I am not letting you speak. That's the case with me. I generally don't allow the other person to speak until I am out of words but since you look like a gentleman I can be little lenient with you but that would be also be in a form of a challenge. How can you end this conversation without being rude?"

"We reached" Rishabh said humbly, smiling and pointing towards the hotel Courtyard Marriot.

"Oh shit you won," she said jumping out of the car and then came back, "Hey you should stay till the event ends. Then let's grab some coffee together and begin the next round of conversation."

"One way conversation," Rishabh expounded.

"Yes an interesting one way conversation in recent times. But don't worry, I will let you speak in round two," she expatiated further.

"Okay," Rishabh said and handed over the key to the valet.

"Why are we here by the way?" Rishabh enquired as they entered the hotel.

"To do some good work. They say money takes away the mental peace. Let's give them some peace by making them little lighter on their pockets."

The event was an exhibition of the paintings that were on

23

sale. The people who came over there were glittering like diamonds draped in expensive clothes and accessories. Some of them were true art lovers while others came to flaunt the size of their bank accounts. Some were humble while others were ballooned with pride of their ancestral inheritance of wealth. The paintings were spread across the walls of the hall to be clearly visible to everyone. The glittering diamonds walked with a haughty gait and drinks in their hands. In that spurious milieu where ego was triumphing in every corner of the hall, the truth lied in the paintings and in the eyes of Rishabh which were stuck on her animated hands, her vacillating hair, her playful eyes, her enigmatic smile, her amazing fragrance. Every glimpse of her made Rishabh content for being in this world and in parallel raised his desire of exploring more of her beauty. One blink could have cost a loss of opportunity to witness another miracle of God.

She walked towards a painting which was being analyzed and stared at by a *bald and bellyful* guy since long.

"Beautiful, isn't it?" she said looking at the painting which was of a lady in a bathtub with clothes on. "The name of the painting is *bloody bathtub* and the painter is a recluse so I represent it on his behalf."

"It's beautiful but the painter should have expressed his feelings openly. I mean who imagines a lady in a bathtub with clothes on," he said. Each of his words was encrypted with 'LU' in the beginning and 'ST' in the end. His bald head and golden tooth made him the most glistening diamond of the evening.

"Oh it's a very painful painting. If you would have known the story behind this, you would have never said that."

"What story?"

"Story of a dreamer who dreams of a bathtub."

"A bathtub?"

"Yes a bathtub. She lives in a small shack in a slum. When people like us feel miserable at a loss of an internet connection, her fight begins with the first light of the morning as she opens her eyes."

Rishabh's ears were now also on a full-fledged work after his eyes. He caught her each and every word like a highly trained wicket keeper who never misses a ball near his gloves.

"While most of us complain about Monday mornings she wakes up at the dawn every day and embraces the struggle like a long lost love. At the tender age of eight, she doesn't even understand what the struggle is? She accepted it as a way of life. Her shack was like seat number 32 of a train compartment from where both the lavatories are at equal distance. So she had to travel half a kilometer everyday just to attend the nature's call. After finishing her own household work, she had to carry a small kid and go for begging. Seventy percent of her earnings went to a local goon. Even with those remaining thirty percent she had power packed dreams, unlike most of us who are even afraid of dreaming. Her paralyzed father, abusive mother, drug addict brother were just other harsh realities of her life. Within all the clutter whenever she got time she would go and stand outside a TV showroom and get happy by watching whatever there was on a display. In one of those frequent visits to a TV showroom, one day she saw a bathtub and she was fascinated with the idea of taking a bath in something like that. Every night she would imagine herself going inside a bathtub and sinking in. The more she went inside the water, the lesser the pain. She wanted to hide in that bathtub, water numbed the pain while hiding. She knew one day she will stop getting up early. One day she will wake up not to work but just to take a bath, in that bathtub."

Several others gathered around that painting by now. Angel successfully generated the vicarious sympathies towards that specious lady in the bath tub. Tears started rolling out of that bald diamond. She gave him a tissue paper. After gaining some control he said, "What happened next?"

"As time passed, life only got tougher. At sixteen she was dragged into prostitution. She hated every single day of being a grown up. She felt she was much happy when she was small. Society abused her, every day she felt worse than yesterday. Those monsters treated her body like a bag of meat. If that was not enough, her family would do the rest. Her drug addict brother would make her pay to the goons for his fiddles. Her father passed away but left behind the money lenders. Her mother became severely ill now and her medication cost went up every day."

He used all the tissue papers she gave him and he was still crying and saying "What happened next?" Rishabh on the other hand was mentally smiling at Angel's glibness.

"Some people's sufferings never end. It's like they are forbidden and then forgotten by the God. Her brother got killed in a gang war. Her mother also passed away one day. She was broke to the core. She cried like no one before. Whatever emotions she had because of her family were also shattered. She was all alone now. She started spending a non-humane life until one day she came across a lavatory store while walking down the street. What she saw at the entrance was like a pulse to the dead. It was a bathtub. She looked at it with moist eyes for minutes before entering into the showroom. She had a vivid recollection of her gory past which made her weak. Gaining some strength she went inside the store. Before any salesman could attend her, she stepped inside the bathtub which was filled with water for display. She let herself sink in while everyone watched and laughed at her. That's when our painter saw her."

The story brought tears to everyone eyes who heard her, except Rishabh.

"What is the cost of this painting?" the bald man asked, still crying.

"Five lakhs Sir," she replied.

"Will this amount help the lady also?"

"Yes Sir"

"I will pay ten then"

Everyone clapped in the room. The bald man took out his cheque book, filled in the details at the payment desk and asked for the painter.

"The painter is a recluse as I said. He never shows up and doesn't like to reveal his name too."

"Some people are so modest of their talent," he exclaimed.

"Exactly Sir."

"So how do I pay him?"

"You can give the cheque to me. I will pay him. You can trust me. I have my details with this hotel." The guy at the payment desk nodded to the bald guy. After that, who could not trust that beauty?

She collected the cheque and signaled Rishabh for leaving.

Soon the Porsche started rolling. "So you are a con artist?" Rishabh concluded.

"Bingo. That was really fast Jason. Take left," she said, unruffled.

From wide roads to narrow streets to a dead end, the black beauty carrying two intelligent asses came to a halt at a shabby place.

They walked into a small house which had just one room and occupied five members, a handicapped guy, a withered woman, two teenaged girls and a toddler. The moment they saw Angel, their faces lighted up with a megawatt smile. The toddler started jumping. Angel had an inherent quality of spreading smiles and happiness.

"How are you Rehmaan chacha?" Angel asked a middle aged guy sitting on a chair.

"I am good," Chacha (uncle) replied with a humble smile. "These girls were talking about you only right now," he said gesturing towards the girls who were smiling ear to ear in the presence of their Angel Didi (elder sister).

"Really? Sharfun, Nafisa, come here."

She hugged them both and gave them a cheque to give to their father.

"What is this Angel beta?"

"Your earnings out of that painting. Now you don't have to worry about Sharfun and Nafisa's education."

"ANGEL," Rishabh's brain echoed the name after hearing it for the first time along with being amazed at what was happening. The con artist turned out to be a lady Robinhood.

The four of them could not stop crying and smiling at the same time. The toddler could not stop jumping. They fed Rishabh and Angel with whatever there was in the kitchen. There are always free meals in the positive world. After receiving tons of thanks from the family they both started walking towards the Porsche.

Rishabh was spellbound with this God's creation called Angel. At first look, she was beautiful but now even Shakespeare uncle would surrender to describe her beauty. She was beautiful, she was smart and she was caring. Who would not fall in love with her? Rishabh was just human. After a long time Rishabh felt something real and that feeling was extremely pure and powerful. There are very few truths in this world and when you come across one, you know it, you recognize it, and you embrace it. Rishabh experienced those true feelings towards Angel.

She was the epitome of every positive adjective Rishabh knew of. She was beautiful inside out. She was the Himalayan water, the fresh oxygen of the forest, the waterfalls of Western Ghats and Deccan plateau. For thirty seconds of that sixty second walk from Rehmaan Chacha's home to Porsche, Rishabh's thoughts were flying exuberantly and then one cruel thought killed all others. *'What if she is married or committed?'* the cruel thought hit him. And then the Sherlock part of Rishabh's brain took over.

"No rings, no mangalsutra (wedding necklace), no Sindoor (vermillion), no accessories," Rishabh started practicing science of deduction. Indian women wear some accessories after marriage and it is easy to recognize a married Indian woman. *"But what if she or her family is iconoclast and don't believe in such traditions. What if she is a free bird?"* Rishabh's mental masturbation began.

"Fuck Sherlockism. She is not married and I am going to express my feelings today," he thought obdurately.

Sometimes when your dream is big enough, facts don't

count. You become so adamant in realizing your dreams that nothing matters.

"*But what if she is committed to someone already?*" Rishabh's Sherlockism started again.

"*She is one of those rare breeds who prefer to be in the company of smart, intelligent, honest and mature guys and she looks of around twenty five. Twenty five plus or minus five aged smart, intelligent, honest and mature guys are rarest of the rare breeds so chances of her being committed are almost reduced to 0.*"

"*Really?*" he asked himself. Sometimes the mental masturbation gets fierce.

"*Fuck Sherlockism. She is not committed and I am going to share my feelings at any cost.*"

"SAY IT," Angel almost shouted at Rishabh.

While Rishabh was fucking his brains off, Angel's shattering voice made him wear his mental pants quickly.

"What? Are you Professor X?" Rishabh asked her instantly in astonishment, wondering whether she is really a mutant.

"I don't need to be someone from X-men to infer the obvious. I just helped someone and I do it regularly for myself. It gives me huge contentment and with selfish interest I keep doing it but people think it is some great work and they are enthused about me, they appreciate me a lot which is pretty normal but you haven't said a single word since long which is not normal, which means there is something else on your mind and I am not able to decipher it. So say it, please," Angel ejaculated in one go leaving Rishabh perplexed at her speech, her swinging hair, her waving duppata (long scarf worn over Indian outfits), her beautiful hands, her highly expressive eyes, her moving lips.

30

Even looking at her should have been charged by her parents for producing the most amazing production. If they can charge for Taj Mahal, why not Angel?

"There is a coffee shop nearby. They say saying things over there create great sayings. Shall we?" the writer released a cupid's arrow which after hitting the target resulted in a most amazing smile of the century.

"Let's roll," she said.

They reached on an open terrace coffee shop away from hustle and bustle of the city, a perfect place for two young people to get attracted to each other and fall in love.

"So what do you do Jason?" she asked.

"Rishabh," Rishabh snapped instantly.

"Okay Jason. I heard your name. Now tell me what do you do?"

Smiling at her blitheness Rishabh answered, "I meet people, drink coffee and mint money."

"Then hire me. I will make you a billionaire if you are a millionaire," she was like a plane which could take off from anywhere, reposefully intellectual conversations included. "If human bodies were filled with coffee I would have become a vampire already. Smell of the coffee is an aphrodisiac for me. But your drinking coffee and minting money logic is beyond my understanding unless you have some super digestive system which gives you the super power of drinking coffee and you know what. But in that case there must be a bank locker in place of a commode in your house."

Rishabh was amused by her creative verbose. He added some more fuel to her creative engine to enjoy the ride further, "So how did you escape from that research center where the most beautiful, intelligent and innocuous aliens are kept for studies."

"Oh they were all high on a party of a father alien and a mother alien. That small prematurely born baby alien told me that it was like Ethan Hunt's self-destructive devices sent by the Almighty to tell me that I have 10 minutes to escape. So I got my signal and ran away. Later on I heard that the baby alien ate himself up."

Rishabh laughed heartily this time. After getting stable he asked her, "Would you like to have some cookies? They make world class cookies here."

"Yes of course if they help us to reveal your profession."

"I am a.."

"Oh wait," She interrupted him as if something occurred to her suddenly. "I think just the thought of cookies have started working. You look very mature in your talking. You have spoken very little but your selection of words is incredible, the costly pen inside your blazer pocket, the hank moody bracelet, the dictionary, and few books on the back seat. And most important thing, the coffee, the fuel for an artist. And now I remember your name also. You are Rishabh, the writer, right?"

"Just a writer but you young lady are a charmer, an enchanter, a helper, a fighter, Sherlocker, Holmer, what noter. You are a bomber woman. You explode positivity wherever you go."

Waiter came in the scene and asked, "Anything else Sir," to which Angel replied, "Two more coffee and few of those world class cookies. I think this conversation is going to last a little longer."

They kept on talking and walking steps towards each other's hearts. It was not a conversation between two bodies;

it was a conversation between two souls.

"So Mr. Writer, you always write someone else's story. What's your story?"

"How do you manage to ask normal questions like normal people?"

"Yeah that's one of my hidden traits plus they give me normalcy shots. So being normal, asking normal questions is manageable. And now please don't change the topic. I want to hear your love story."

"My love story?" Rishabh asked, a bit puzzled about the fact that the story had just begun.

"Yes I have read your books Rishabh and you seem to be a romantic person," she said and then decreased the volume of her voice, "I also love the way you describe intimate scenes."

Rishabh smiled sheepishly.

"Oh come on. Don't be a spoilsport. You want some more coffee. They have a tank full of it. And if you will not tell me right away, I will shout aloud that you are gay, right now in front of everyone."

Rishabh gave thumbs up and she instantly stood up on the chair.

"Hellooooooo everyone. Please pay attention here," she started shouting to gain the attention of people nearby. "This gentleman here sitting in front of me.." Before she could say anything else, Rishabh stood up and pulled her down, "Okay, okay, I will tell you. Please sit down."

Angel started laughing and Rishabh smiled sheepishly again.

"Your normalcy shot doesn't work for longer durations. You need more of that."

"Okay I am all ears and all the people here are all eyes on me so you better start talking what I want to hear."

Rishabh was going crazy after her spontaneity and flamboyance but maintaining his veneer of normalcy he said, "Angel, I am a writer and it would be best if I present my love story to you through my writing. So I promise before the day ends, you will have it," he said and took a sip of coffee.

"angelicajokha at gmail dot com"

Rishabh laughed suddenly saving the coffee in his mouth to spill on the table after discovering her innovative email id.

"Before that it was angelinabinajina and big cross after that at gmail dot com."

Rishabh laughed more. He felt ecstatic.

"You know you are witty, you are funny, you have an amazing heart which craves for selfless help to the people in need. A thesis should be written on your sense of humor, your spontaneity and the way you carry on conversation. You hate to be appreciated for the work you do because you believe that helping others should be a common thing, why make a hustle about it? You are a free soul like a blowing wind or flowing water, no attachments. And the most important thing about you is that you are beautiful inside out and you don't take any pride in it."

A silently smiling Angel looked equally beautiful to Rishabh. She kept smiling listening to her own description. Before the silence could turn awkward, she spoke.

"Well! That was very directly from heart, no additives. Thanks."

"May I ask you something?" he asked as he found the stage set to throw the million dollar question.

"Shoot", she gave the permission.

"Who is the lucky guy?"

"Why do you want to know?"

"To tell my girl how she was on the verge of losing her boyfriend in a cafe."

She smiled noticing his obvious bluff and replied, "The guy is yet to be lucky."

And that sparkling eye contact lasted more than the usual time.

4

Rishabh's writing table was very simple. A lexicon, a laptop, a diary, a pen holder and a message on the wall in front that said, 'The world witnessed some best written words after a rigorous fighting with a blank page for hours.'

Rishabh's fingers started hitting the keyboard. For the first time he was so sure about each and every word he was typing as if he was born to write that letter, as if he was preparing for that letter from past few births.

Dear Angel,

You know me as a writer but let me confess that writing does not come easy to me. I combat the blank screen for the most of my time but today words are coming easy, may be because I met that girl today.

She is nuts, a total maniac. She creates an adventurous ride wherever she goes. She helps animals, she controls traffic, she supports the needy and damn she is so beautiful.

So we got into this amazing conversation. Her talks kept flowing like a river while my thirst kept on increasing with each savored sip. I knew it then and there that I want to make it a life time exercise of quenching my thirst.

The way she makes me smile is highly neurotic. Her extremely expressive eyes take me to the freedom-land where I get free rides of blissfulness. I have never been so sure about anyone. She is the one. You are the one, Angel.

I don't know about your feelings for me and I don't want to waste time trying to figure it out in a roundabout manner that is why I am writing this letter just after our first meeting. I have this feeling that any tiny delay from side can drift us certain degrees apart and we will get lost out there which scares the shit out of me because we always miss a lot of moments every day, moments which could have shaped our life exactly the way we wanted. I don't know whether we will be together or not, whether I will become your lucky guy or not, but damn you smell good and we both like coffee, which calls for something.

And yes that's my love story, the beginning actually.

Waiting for your reply.

Rishabh

He typed angelicajokha@gmail.com in front of the To tab and pressed send button but a pop up came on the screen saying the mail is without the subject.

Now Rishabh was a visionary. He practiced the secret, law of attraction a lot. He thought of a period when they both would be together, scanning older mails. What if they found their first email and with that thought he immediately started typing in front of the subject tab, *Coffee pours heart out*. He pressed the send button.

Thinking that Angel would take time to reply, he connected his laptop with speakers at full volume so that reply from her even at late night should wake him up in case he snoozes. His cell phone, his tablet, all the gadgets were on a high-speed internet and at a full volume.

The moment he sat on the chair thinking about her, a shrieking *tiding* sound from speakers generated a jerk inside him thereby making him fall from the chair. A moment later, mobile phone and tablet also shouted and Rishabh was like, "*I know, I know, keep quiet.*" He did not waste time in arranging the chair. Standing on his knees he clicked on the reply from Angel which said, "Find me and don't waste time on social media."

She knew Rishabh would email her and she wanted him to find her without giving any clues. She never missed a chance to fill the adventure, the most essential ingredient of her spicy life. The more Rishabh knew about her the more he fell for her.

After reading the reply, Rishabh's brain started scanning the events and searching for clues. He knew that any person on the planet could be reached via six connections.

"Who was the first connection?" he thought and it instantly clicked "*Rehmaan chacha.*"

Rishabh's laptop showed 8:12 pm and at 8:24 pm he was at Rehmaan chacha's home savoring delicious *gajar ka halwa* (Indian sweet dish).

There are three categories of people in a person's life based on which the information is taken out. Number one is the hot category. They can take a bullet for you, so can you for them. They know your dark secrets, so do you of them. If Armageddon is about to happen and you have immunity potion with you, you will give them to your hots. Now these hots can give you any information of the world they have by asking them just once. If they are working inside the white house and they know the dark secrets, they will share it with you.

Number two is a warm category. There is a well-constructed bridge between you two. To get the information all you need to do is travel that bridge first, hug them and ask what you want. So this category will take some promises from you and then share whatever they know.

Number three is cold. There is no bridge. It needs to be constructed first and Rehmaan chacha was Rishabh's cold category. Rishabh gained his emotional quotient by observing people and their situations. Rishabh knew how to build that bridge. He spoke to Rehmaan chacha and appreciated his painting. He spoke to his family one by one, with his wife, his daughters and played with the toddler. The interaction became very warm with earthly nature of Rishabh. Rehmaan chacha found him to be a Good Samaritan so he interacted more and finally asked him the million dollar question.

"How do you know Angel?"

When you are on a mission, the first victory is very important. It gives you a power booster. It brings you one step closer to your goal.

"Rehmaan Chacha I really don't know her yet. We met this morning but I don't remember a single moment of the day when I have not thought about her. She has a great heart and it's like God has sent her here to introduce us with heaven. I want to know more about her and that's why I came here. She didn't tell me where she stays but she sent an email saying 'find me'."

Rehmaan chacha smiled hearing good words about Angel and watching Rishabh's honesty.

"She truly is an angel of the Almighty," he said. "Inshallah you both should meet very soon but son I too don't know her address. It was a month ago when my elder daughter Sharfun met with a road accident and it was Angel who helped her and got her treated. Last week when she came here to ask about her health, she came to know about our financial condition and today she came up with ten lakh rupees. I really don't know how to repay her debt."

"I know where she stays?" Sharfun jumped in, breaking Rishabh's pensive mode.

"Where?" Rishabh asked with a great anticipation.

"Gandhinagar"

"How do you know that?"

"Her vehicle number is GJ18PC3108"

Rishabh was beatified by her intelligence.

"Almighty has given her very good power of memorizing things," Rehmaan chacha said.

"Apart from memorizing she is also very good at general knowledge," Rishabh corroborated.

He kissed the toddler and greeted everyone. "Here is my card. Please don't shy away from calling me anytime."

"But Gandhinagar is huge. How will you find her, Rishabh bhaiya," Sharfun asked in her innocent voice.

He smiled and said, "You are very intelligent Sharfun. You know before I met you, Angel could be anywhere in this huge world but now I know she is somewhere in that small city called Gandhinagar. I can easily find her now. Kudos to you dear."

He jumped into his convertible without opening the door and directed his chariot towards Courtyard Marriot hotel.

An utterly beautiful, hot and sexy five feet seven inches tall receptionist welcomed Rishabh with an electric smile, "How may I help you Sir?" to which he replied by flaunting his skills. "Well you can make me a billionaire by telling me that thousand year old hidden secret of being so beautiful but that would be too big a favor to ask for the first meeting."

Rishabh had this innate quality of making people take off

40

the mask and being real.

"What do you want?" she asked with a smirk.

"I am a writer and I am searching someone whom I can envisage a character of my story."

"Wow. I always fantasize about being on a date with a writer who keeps on praising me for a whole night."

"Well that looks like a great date, a very tempting one indeed but I think I am going to book myself to someone for next few births in next few hours."

"You just broke my heart sweetheart."

"I know it's not very gentlemanly but I would do anything to mend it."

The lady contemplated a little and then asked, "Are you Rishabh?"

"Are you some secret service agent playing a role of receptionist?"

"Oh come on, that was not so difficult. I have seen your picture on the back cover of your book. You have a photogenic face. By the way I love your writing."

"My four most favorite words of the English language. Genuinely ecstatic to hear that."

"What's the name of your search?"

"Angel. She was representing the painting called bloody bathtub in today's painting exhibition."

"Okay," she said and started scanning the screen in front of her. A minute later she replied, "Sorry handsome, no address, its only sector 22 mentioned here. The guy in the morning shift must have saved her documents but I can't locate them right now. You will have to come again in the morning sweetheart."

"Lady you cannot even imagine what a great help you

have extended towards me. Don't be sorry, in fact I owe you a treat but not at this time, some other day. Thank you so much," he said and went like a typhoon.

The roads of Gandhinagar became an F1 lap for Porsche. Thirty five kilometers were covered in just fifteen minutes. Rishabh scanned sector 22 for almost twenty two times but no result. He settled down for a while on a side of a lonely road. In fact at just 10 pm the whole sector 22 looked lonely and spooky.

He was sitting on a bonnet with his arms wrapped around his knees.

'How can someone like Angel stay at such a quiet place?' Rishabh thought.

Suddenly an off white skinned stray dog started barking at him. Rishabh searched his pockets and found those left over world class cookies inside them. He threw one in the air towards the four-legged loving mammal and it was smartly caught by the athletic creature. Then he placed the rest on the bonnet. The canine jumped on the bonnet and ate those. Rishabh rubbed its back and it instantly settled down on bonnet besides Rishabh wiggling its tail. Animals do not wear mask so Rishabh did not need words this time.

"How were the cookies?" Rishabh asked and the dog started licking his pants. He made it calm down by rubbing its back and neck.

"Dude it looks like you know this area well." The dog stood up showing his confidence.

"Please don't get me wrong but I am searching a girl of your area. We met this morning." He lowered his tail wiggling in slow movements showing confusion.

"She has this tendency to make us all go crazy for her.

You know she is like you, she also did not eat the whole cookie." He looked at Rishabh with eyes wide open as if asking "Who ate the remaining?"

"Of course I did," Rishabh said, "After she left," he finished.

"You know it's more than love," he continued sharing his feelings. "Like I love you too but the way I feel for her, it's so different, so unique. It's about the feeling of what to do or say next to make her smile. Although she does most of that part but making her smile feels like a responsibility to me." The dog sat down moving his tongue like a kid listening to a story from granny.

"Her smell, damn she smells so good. I think she plays a key role in the research and development of all the perfume industries. It's like she is a goddess of fragrance. You know in front of you also I remember her smell. By the way when did you take the bath last?" Canine shook his head negatively.

"I want to meet her parents and congratulate them for such an amazing result of their work. I want to ask them what were they thinking during her inception, what were the emotions like? Did they have their honeymoon in heaven? And the name. How did they already know that she is exactly going to be an Angel?"

The name echoed in the dog's ears. He stood up instantly and started wiggling his tail furiously. He jumped off the bonnet and started shaking his whole body.

"What happened?" Rishabh asked. "Don't tell me that in this abandoned looking sector 22 I have found an informer who can tell me where does the Angel stay?"

He raised his front legs and moved in forward direction.

"*Je baat*. Let's go my friend," Rishabh said triumphantly and jumped on the seat putting the Porsche back on power.

The dog stopped in front of a bungalow. Rishabh parked his car at a distance, stepped out and started walking towards the bungalow. It was 10:30pm and Gandhinagar had worn the blanket of silence. Rishabh scanned the bungalow. It was a two storey building, a black gate, a small lawn in front, a parked car and a two wheeler and a balcony. While Rishabh was lost in the thoughts of a movie scene where hero climbs up on a balcony through some pipe and jumps into a heroine's room, suddenly a rapid figure held Rishabh's hand from behind and said, "Run, run, run." It was Angel. They started running and the dog followed. Rishabh was enthralled with what took hold of him.

Gandhinagar is lush green. It is also known as the green city. Trees are planted at an equal distance from each other so it generates an eye-catching pattern. Now in that pattern there was a certain location which gets hidden from most of the angles and with the dark in place the location was a hideout. Angel and Rishabh reached the location along with the canine.

"This is my favorite hideout since childhood," Angel said.

"So you knew I will come and you were waiting for me," Rishabh said smiling ear to ear.

"Of course, but I did not know that you would take help of Nelson for this," she said looking at the dog who was moving sporadically around them.

"Oh Nelson," Rishabh said looking at him. "Yes indeed the genius turned out to be a rockstar of tonight. Had he not been there, I would not have reached the person on whom the whole moonlight is falling right now. I am highly confused with a baffling thought of whether you look more beautiful during the day or at the night?"

"And the cheapest flirting award goes to Rishabh. Yayyyyyy," she said clapping slowly.

"I can be cheap like this for my whole life and still feel like the richest person on this planet."

She held his hand firmly. "You know Rishabh, I have seen guys say things to me but you are the master of all. You have this ability to make people feel special about themselves which I have seen your characters doing in your books too. And everything with you feels so real and truthful." Without even realizing, they came very close to each other. Nelson started wiggling his tail in rapid movements.

"I want to ask you something" Rishabh said.

"What is it?"

"Why did you make me run here?"

"You want to know?"

"More than the biggest secret of the universe"

"To properly give a reply to your e-mail"

"And that is?"

Angel smiled with a twinkle in her eyes. She brought Rishabh closer and landed her lips on his. Nelson was jumping in the air by now.

"I love you too," she replied after kissing.

With closed eyes he kept smiling without saying a word.

"Will you say something?" she asked.

"The holy feeling, the divine power. I just felt I got my kundalini awakening. Was that a kiss or a tickle from God?"

"Stop hallucinating," Angel laughed. "And just run and go now," she said and started walking.

"What? No whatsapp? No facebook?

"They are fun killers and for impatient people and I have heard that writers are very patient," she said while walking. Rishabh followed.

"Of course. I will then wait for the whole night to pick you up in the morning."

"No need"

"Then how and where are we going to meet again?"

"Let's get caffeinated tomorrow morning," she said and walked away. Rishabh kept staring without blinking till she disappeared in that bungalow. He then very quietly got into his car and left from there.

In this love story things were moving fast but they both were so sure about each other that fast seemed illogical. It looked like they were bound to meet and fall in love. It's like saying Rajkumar Hirani movie will do a good business. What an illogical statement that would be? Of course it will do a good business. Destiny was hundred percent sure of bringing them together. And like Rishabh, all the Hindu deities above the cloud were waiting for the next morning.

5

For Rishabh fashion meant black shirt or a black tee over denim blue pants. The only addition at times was a black Prada blazer. When someone once asked him about the reason for his love for black and blue he gave a classic reply.

"Words define me. They are my asset, my life. I am the words and most of them can be seen in black and blue."

Rishabh was a successful writer but to become one he went through a process which every successful person goes through. Following your dream or pursuing your passion takes everything. You have to risk everything. It might break you mentally and financially. Getting up again after every small failure might need a lot of strength. You might get tempted to go back to your past life where you traded security against your freedom but if you can shut off that loud temptation under the voice of your own heartbeat which says, '*Just one more step*' after every time you fall down, that's when success gets attracted and run towards you to hug you tightly. In the end, everything is worth it. More than money, successful and financially free people spend time the way they want. They spend it lavishly and that's what Rishabh was doing. On Tuesday morning during rush hour he was enjoying every second of the wait for Angel at an open terrace cafe.

And when she entered in a sea green top and black jeans, not only Rishabh but the whole arena of the cafe including whole staff seemed to be awestruck at her radiance, the positive vibes started a marathon from her to everywhere.

Rishabh got up to greet her. They both hugged each other, communicating without a word in a way that said *"Last night did not pass so easy"*

"Sorry I am late," she said, admitting the mistake with the cutest smile ever.

"No, you are stunning," Rishabh's testosterone levels were touching the percentage of a gold medalist of a university since last night.

"And you are flirting," she said.

"Just obliging to what my heart says"

The manager of the cafe came to their table wearing an ostentatious smile, "Sir, today is the first anniversary of our cafe and since you are our first customer today, we will not bill your order."

"Yo man," Angel got up and gave a pat on manager's shoulder. "In that case, I will make the coffee for the whole staff today"

Angel had this super power of amplifying the sanguinity. She was the brand ambassador of *'Vasudhaiva Kutumbakam'* treating everyone as a family. Before manager could say anything she treaded towards kitchen, shook hands and congratulated everyone there and started to show her culinary skills.

First encounter of anyone with Angel was always shocking. It took time for the manager to come out of the shock and stop Angel but Rishabh kept him busy.

"Don't worry Amit, your wife will not know about your affair."

The heavily charged body of the manager running towards the kitchen suddenly faced an immediate brake, and the emergency signals received through the statement of Rishabh brought all bodily programs of Amit, the manager to a halt.

The pop up questions were:

'How does he know my name?'

'How does he know about my affair?'

'What damage can he cause me?'

'Why on the earth did I come to greet these two idiots?'

"Come, sit down. I am your friend," Rishabh pacified him. "And don't worry. She will not cause any damage, neither to your kitchen, nor to your job. Come, let's talk."

He sat with heavy steps. "Who are you?" he asked, flummoxed.

"Rishabh," Rishabh replied humbly.

"How do you know about me?"

"Last evening I heard your conversation with your wife in which you said you will be late because of work and not to prepare the dinner for you. And then you immediately started leaving. Unfortunately, I was also leaving and then downstairs I saw a young lady calling you Amit and hugging and kissing you."

Amit heard him with his mouth open because Rishabh's words became Ninja warriors fighting and placing hurdles for oxygen going towards Amit's respiratory system. Those few oxygen molecules which somehow managed to reach Amit's body made him say, "So you are an accidental intruder in my life."

"Yes, but I am absolutely harmless to you. I don't even know your wife. But I know this lady in the kitchen. Unlike you and me who came on this planet just to intake oxygen, release carbon dioxide, excrete a lot and create a total havoc by using our useless brain, her intentions are very much clear. She wants to make everyone around happy. She is a happy soul and from yesterday till eternity I am the guardian of this soul. So let her do what she is doing and you better focus on your wife rather than that girl. Anyways, she is materialistic and using you as her ATM."

"Bullshit. She loves me."

"No she doesn't. She loves your plastic cards. She was appreciating your clothing, the perfume you were wearing, your car and what not. I even heard you both going for shopping for her. And wait a minute, this phony love is also in the picture? Dude, the problem is deeper then. I thought it was only physical, not emotional. Now I also know that the mirror that I just showed to you, will appear sham to you. So I need to give you a demo. Everybody needs a demo, you are no different. Give me your phone."

And like a hypnotic patient, he handed over his phone to Rishabh whose Sherlockism was on fire. Rishabh checked his call log and found a number saved with an ambiguous name *Jelly*, the only odd name out of all the calls made in last one day. He dialed it, put the phone on speaker and waited for someone to answer.

"Hey jaanu, the Versace bag is just awesome. Thank you so much. Love you sweetheart," someone thanked her ATM.

"Your sweetheart is a drug addict and he is in our custody," Rishabh stated in a firm voice. "He owns us one lakh rupees."

"So?" she became repulsive instantly. "Call his wife. Why are you calling me?"

"Fucking bitch," Amit said in a loudest mute volume.

"He says you love him and understand him. You only can help him in this situation without getting a bad name."

"Tell him he is a bloody loser and I don't even know him. Don't call me again or else I will report you" and the call gets disconnected.

Rishabh handed over the phone. "Now please don't start sulking like a little girl. Just call your wife and tell her that you love her."

But some people just don't listen. He did not call his wife.

And he started sulking.

Yes, like a little girl.

He started sobbing and speaking at the same time, "She is a bitch."

"I know"

"You are a savior"

"I know that too"

"I am truly grateful to you. Thank you so much brother."

"Come here. Let's hug it out. And stop crying. Angel should not watch you like this"

They hugged. Angel arrived and the manager left.

"Was he crying?" Angel asked.

"He was talking about his failed investments. I gave him a solution so he was just being thankful and got emotional and you know it just occurred to me that you are looking so beautiful today, just like yesterday."

She beamed and placed her arms around Rishabh's shoulders. The eyes locked instantly and the magnetism of both the bodies was so high that it caused a high level of mutual induction, generating tremendous voltage to bring the lips closer and closer but some morons just don't understand the science and interrupt the beautiful process.

"The coffee was amazing mam," the waiter said. "Everyone loved it. We have asked our manager to put it on the menu card and he agreed to it instantly. He is otherwise a very strict boss but today he yielded to our request very easily. Can you please suggest us the name for the coffee?"

"Crangel café," Rishabh said.

"Thank you Sir," waiter said and left.

"Crangel?" Angel asked in question.

"Crazy Angel"

"You are so adorable while coining a word."

"And you are smoking. I love your smell"

The scientific process was about to begin again but another moron interrupted in between.

"Your Crangel café," waiter said bringing a tray and placing it on a table.

"I don't think they will let you kiss me today," Angel said teasing Rishabh.

"No worries. Kiss you later. Smell you till then."

Sometimes spoilers just don't cease. Angel's phone started ringing on the table. At first she gave a cutest angry look at it and when she saw the number on display she started smiling and rubbing her hands in anticipation to another adventure. It was an unknown number and she loved to talk strange things with strangers. She picked up the phone.

"Hello," Angel said.

"Beta I am Neetu aunty. Is Reshma there?"

"No aunty Reshma has gone for her pre-marital honeymoon but she said you have an appointment for today. So when are you coming for your bikini photo shoot?"

Rishabh tried to control his laughter gauging her prank quickly.

"What nonsense? Who are you?"

"I am Billo, Reshma's assistant. If you are not comfortable with bikini, Billo can arrange a swimsuit for you or a bodice. Trust me, you husband will buy you some costly jewelries after watching your pictures in that. We have recently started a spa service. Your body will be treated so gently and professionally that your husband will go crazy after you. Your sex life will be spiced up again."

The call went dead leaving the two of them in hysterics. The manager and the staff joined them too.

"You never miss any opportunity, do you?"

"Anything else you want to order Sir?" Waiter interrupted again.

"The only thing I am missing right now is few private moments with you," she told Rishabh. "Come on, come on, we need to go somewhere. Let's go," Angel said.

"But where?"

"Come oooon. Hurry up," she grabbed his arm and started running.

It was a huge terrace and café was on just one corner. She took him to the other corner. She started sitting on a boundary wall of terrace.

"Careful," Rishabh said while giving her a hand.

She sat comfortably. "Come, sit," she said.

Rishabh climbed up and sat, little uncomfortable.

Ahmedabad doesn't have high rise buildings but even an

eight storey building looks like Burj Khalifa when you are sitting on a boundary wall.

"Isn't it too high for the normal ones?" Rishabh asked.

"Are you scared?"

"Oh no, absolutely not. I just don't want to shit my pants in front of the lady I love."

Angel chuckled. "Chill, give me your hand," she soothed him and held his hand.

Now that was a riding feeling for Rishabh, a roller coaster ride where you are little scared and highly thrilled. The blowing wind above and moving traffic below, which create physical and mental imbalance at heights, was mollified by the soft touch of Angel. Every cell of her hand was so positively charged that Rishabh's mental and physical balance was instantly restored. It was magical.

They sat there for few minutes holding each other's hand savoring the top view of Ahmedabad. Angel looked surreal in silence. May be these were her moments where she created the sphere of silence around her and charged herself. Silence has amazing powers. It can do wonders. It helps to unleash the hidden powers of a human being.

"What are you thinking?" Rishabh asked.

"Just small little things?"

"That's exactly where life is hidden, rest everything is a hoax. Can you please take me inside your head, the Disneyland of adults?"

Angel looked at Rishabh, smirked and then started looking at the traffic below.

"Why have we created such a system where people have to run so hard?" An office employee was running after a bus, his body language shouting loudly that he was horribly late.

Angel started unveiling her deepest hidden thoughts.

"A system where we don't trust each other." An auto rickshaw driver was brawling with a biker.

"A system where we do not spare a minute to show some care to a poor kid. How much time does it take to make friendship with that kid and just say hello to him while passing by the same route every day." A poor kid was asking for some help and everybody was busy looking at their watches and running towards the unknown treasury of no value.

"How did we end up being like this?" Angel said. "When and where it all went wrong? Why someone can't just built a time machine, find where exactly the error occurred in the past and rectify it? I am sure we were not like this in the beginning. Everyone is a pure soul, many of them devoid of happiness today. Like a body needs water, oxygen and food, lack of which creates imbalance, a soul needs happiness, truth, knowledge, peace, purity, love and bliss. Imbalance can be clearly seen in the world today because of the lack of consumption of what a soul needs."

Rishabh placed a hand on her shoulder and brought her closer. "I know we have messed up a lot. I know most of us run after illusionary things, spending most of our precious time on trivial things. God gave us time and energy to find love and happiness but we discovered the likes of money and ruined everything. I know we have corrupted a lot of things on this planet but still this world is a beautiful place to stay. It's because of the people like you who fight with their every breath to restore the balance. One life is worth a visit to witness the magic you create every day." He brought her face closer to his, "I love you Angel," and kissed her forehead. "I thank all the powers of the universe for making me meet you. Passing this journey of life without meeting you would have been a total waste. I love you from the bottom of my heart Angel," and he kissed her. They kissed like crazy, even if they would have fallen from that building they would have kept kissing. It was not just a kiss; it was an ethereal expression denoting a marriage of two souls. They sat there for some more time embracing each other reaching new heights of love, getting high on kiss.

"You want to go somewhere?" Angel asked.

"Yes"

"Where would you like to go?"

"I want to see your daily routine. I want to see your life. I want to see the real Angel in action. Though I have seen a trailer, I want to see the whole movie now. I know you freelance utopian socialism which is your art or skill but how this art form is put into practice, I want to witness that."

"Freelance utopian socialism?" she imitated him jokingly. "How do you coin such words? You writers have a separate lexicon or what?"

"I think socialism is calling you. Shall we?" Rishabh said gesturing his hand for leaving.

"Look, I don't know how you will take it. Things might get awry, you may feel uncomfortable with certain situations."

"Just tell me when you are done with your boring lecture, and then, we will go for some real action."

Angel smiled and felt loved with that gesture of Rishabh.

"Let's run," she said and they both literally started running towards the lift.

"Visit again," the manager said.

They waved while running. Angel took staircase, Rishabh followed. Panting, they both reached the ground floor. A guy kept a water bottle on a reception desk and got engaged in the stock market on a big screen. Angel took the bottle and started drinking. They both moved out of the building.

"Why do you make me run always?"

"To clear the dust in the brain bowl for pouring some nice wine in it."

Rishabh now got used to her fast paced words of wisdom.

"So what's the plan?" Rishabh asked.

"Just chill and keep walking. Hold this bottle, you will feel good. Remember when everyone got up today, they received an equal amount of time from God, but most of them decided to invest that precious gift into something which will never give huge returns, but you have decided to spend it wisely so your returns are going to be huge. Today you are one of those very few on this planet who are filthy rich. So walk like one, okay. Now rich people are mostly humble and helpful but most of them are rich in money so they provide financial aid but you my dear love are rich in time today, so you are going to bestow your time to the needy. Find someone who is depressed or needs help. Make that person smile or offer help whatever you can, thereby planting a seed of humility which in turn will branch out to others converting into a huge humility tree in coming time."

"So now you are a professional networker cum utopian socialist."

Angel smiled with a raised eyebrow and a slow nodding head, "Wow that released a few estrogens and progesterone inside me. You know it just occurred to me, why don't you write an erotic novel?"

"Great thought but lack of experience will make me a poor writer of that topic."

"But the intimate scenes are very well written in your books. Wait. Stop," she made him stop. "Did you just say that you are a virgin?" The passersby became onlookers which was normal in case of Angel.

"I think I said that I am yet to be in touch with one of the strongest emotions ever."

"And here I am, finding someone who needs help," she jibed.

"Was that a statement or a sticker with a loser written on it that you just snapped on me?"

"Oh no, I am really sorry," she said with a chuckle. "And if you feel any better I am a loser too. But you are twenty eight with no sex in life yet."

"Angel," Rishabh said calmly. "Will you please stop hyping up my virginity in public?"

"Hi hottie?" a girl in black glasses, white skin tone and miniskirt asked Rishabh. "I am available for dinner tonight," she smiled.

"But he is not," Angel snapped instantly. "Get lost"

"Fuck you," she said and started walking showing the middle finger.

"Holy kama, why this drama?" Rishabh said melodramatically. "You just snatched a morsel out of the mouth of a poor guy."

"Don't worry, the feast is getting ready for the poor guy," Angel said.

They both kept smiling and looking into each other's eyes.

"Sir, please give me something," a small kid broke their eye contact.

Short pants, torn shirt, disheveled hair, raddled face, the kid looked deplorable which made Rishabh reach out to his wallet but Angel blocked his hand and started chatting with kid.

"What's your name dude?"

"Krishna"

"That's a pretty cool name. Will you be my friend?" Angel asked offering her hand.

The kid looked at Angel for a moment in question but then made a handshake. Rishabh found it amusing how she could ring the bell every time. While any normal person will offer monetary help to such a kid she offered her time and a friendship, the two most precious things than any currency of the world.

"I and Rishabh are very hungry," Angel said. "Krishna, you want to grab some pizza with us?" Angel asked the kid.

Krishna shook his head.

"Alright. We will go to McD and have burger then. You like burgers?" Rishabh asked.

Krishna shook his head again.

"I got it," Angel said. "Krishna loves cakes and pastries. We will go to The Grand bakery."

"No. I don't like pastries," Krishna said.

"Then what do you like?" they both asked in unison.

"Parle-G," Krishna said and they kept looking at him.

Rishabh bought two packets of Parle-G biscuits, one full cup tea and two half cups of tea. They sat on a municipality bench. Rishabh and Angel took one biscuit each, rest were consumed by Krishna.

"Krishna, you want to come and play with us?" Angel asked. "There is a garden nearby. We will go there. Or else we can go to Alpha One mall and play games over there."

"No, I have to gather some money before I go home."

"For what? Dinner?" Rishabh asked him politely.

Krishna got little confused at first but then replied, "No the money is for my mother. She is ill. She needs medicines."

"Fine. Take us to your mother. We will take her to the doctor."

Krishna got confused again and began to see towards a building.

"What happened Krishna? Come on. Let's go. Take us to your mother."

"Do you have a five hundred rupee note?"

Rishabh took out his wallet and gave him the note. Krishna fully opened the note, showed it towards the building and then kept inside his pocket. "Let's go to the garden now. I will give back the note there," he said. What was happening was completely out of their minds. They just followed Krishna towards the garden who was leading them by now.

En route garden was a guy selling lighting toys on roadside. A small kid going along with his mother saw him and demanded the same.

Mother: How much for the toy?

Toy seller: Twenty rupees

Mother understood she could not afford it and started explaining the kid that the toy is not good but he became recalcitrant and started wailing. Angel saw the incident and quickly gave hundred bucks to the toy seller and gave the toy to the kid.

Mother: But madam, I can't afford it. I only have fifty rupees and I have to get vegetables for today.

Angel: Don't worry. It's a gift. I like your kid. He is an adorable kid.

The mother looked at her kid who was playing with the toy and showing it to her mother and grinning a lot. The mother smiled too and thanked Angel. She and her kid went to a construction site nearby.

"Mam, your change," the toy seller said.

"You can keep it but you will have to do some work for me," Angel said.

"Sure mam, what is it?"

She smiled and asked, "What's your name?"

"Abhay," he said.

"Abhay, you look very kind person to me. Today if you find any kid like him, can you please give that kid a toy as a gift? Can you do that for me, please?" she said and placed a hand on his shoulder.

Rishabh saw an instant smile and expression of gratitude on Abhay's face. Abhay thanked her for choosing him to do the good work. And they continued to walk towards the garden along with Krishna.

"How do you do that?" Rishabh asked Angel.

"What?"

"Those expressions were real. I am absolutely sure that he will not cheat, he will definitely give the gifts, but how do you do that? You are just flawless."

"I just try to touch the heart," her redolent words introduced him to another chicanery of that con artist. He was spell bound by that drifting ride where she drifted him away from the normal world.

61

"You are Angel didi right?" Krishna said as they reached the garden.

"Awesome. Now you are a celebrity too," Rishabh said. "That's the best thing about being with you, endless surprises.

"How do you know me Krishna?" Angel asked, all three sitting on a buttery spread thick grass.

"Raheem told me. You fed him when he was really hungry. That day Jaggu bhaiya threw him out in the rain as a punishment."

They both had a lot of questions popped up in their heads but it was obviously Angel who fired up first.

"How is Raheem now?" she asked.

"Oh he is absolutely fine."

"Who is Jaggu bhaiya?"

"He is our manager. He was there in that building to whom I showed the note."

Now Rishabh took the turn. "So your mother is not ill?"

"I don't have a mother," Krishna said. "Nor a father too."

"And you were not hungry too?"

"Who leaves home for work without having food? Do you?" Krishna snapped. "But I can eat a lot, I have a huge capacity," he smiled.

Krishna looked smarter than his age, may be the circumstances made him so. Rishabh and Angel were clear that this whole begging business was being managed by someone. Many articles were afloat on media about the dark world of begging and crime involved behind that, but they were watching the real picture for the first time.

"Why did you say no to pizza and burger then?" Rishabh

asked.

"We are not allowed to go away from the signal until we earn at least five hundred rupees. Also, we are not allowed to eat anything outside other than Parle-G biscuits," Krishna said and then added with a smile, "I like Parle-G, it's better than the food we get there."

"Don't worry Krishna, today you will have the best food in town and no one will come to know about it," Angel said.

"No didi, if Jaggu bhaiya comes to know about it, he will beat me with his belt."

"Before that I will insert a bamboo in his posterior," Angel said furiously.

"Language lady, he is a kid," Rishabh tried to mollify her.

"It's ok bhaiya. I know more bad words than both of you combined," Krishna said. "And didi, please don't do anything. He is a very dangerous man."

"Listen Krishna," Rishabh said, "How many of you are there?"

"We are twenty six. Last night one more came. Now we are twenty seven at this signal. There are many others at other signals," Krishna replied. "I know counting too Angel didi," he said smiling. "They teach us that."

"Krishna, can you gather them at one place? We will take you all out from there," Angel said.

"But they are tough kids. They will never come with you. They hate you all. Their statements begin with mother and end with fucker. Many of them smoke weed too," Krishna said and looked at Rishabh's watch. "What's the time bhaiya?"

"It's twelve fifteen"

"Oh no I need to leave now. Please take your money. I

will give Jaggu bhaiya from my savings. I just wanted to spend some time with Angel didi after Raheem told me so much about her," he said handing over hundred rupee note. Rishabh put it back in his pocket.

"Thank you bhaiya," he said and started running out of the garden.

"I am going to kill this Jaggu," Angel said. "I am going to throw that mother fucker in a chili powder after giving him severe cuts and put the asshole on a hot iron rod. That dickhead is scaring the innocent kids; I am going to scare him to death," she said with the clenched teeth.

Rishabh sighed after listening to her. "You curse dangerously lady."

"Let's go to the police station Rishabh. We have to help these kids anyhow."

"That won't help. They will arrest Jaggu and then leave him on bail. He must have contacts. Our one wrong move will make the children's life worse. Already they are living in hell. We will have to understand the whole setup first. Then and only then can we break it."

"And how can we understand the setup?"

"That you leave up to me princess. Just give me a day; I will get the info out of this jackass Jaggu. Now you just smile and tell me when the feast will be ready?"

Angel beamed, "You will have to buy me a lot of butter to get the feast."

6

Next few days were all about understanding the set up. With the help of Krishna, Rishabh bugged Jaggu. Krishna anyhow fixed a transmitter on Jaggu bhaiya's brown jacket which he wore every day. From abusing to gunfire to moaning, Rishabh heard it all and when the whole picture became clear, Rishabh was shocked.

"Alright, shoot the shit," Angel said to Rishabh. They both were walking near Gandhi Ashram.

"It's worse than we thought. They are running a bloody crime factory."

"Hmm, and these fuckers are using innocent kids as a raw material. How much worse are we talking here by the way?" she asked.

An old lady was trying to cross the road. They held her hands, shut her ears and started to cross the road.

"A lot worse. It all starts right when a kid is born to the poor parents. They rent the infants after a year or so and give them to the female beggars who drug them so that they don't harass them during their shop hours. These female beggars even partner up with milk vendors. They outsmart the smart ones who buy them milk rather than giving money. The milk is then resold to milk vendors at a lower price."

They reached on the other side of the road. "Thank you so much, children," the old lady said. "But why did you shut my ears?"

"We love to talk dirty," Angel whispered in her ear.

The old lady giggled, "Naughty kids. God bless you."

"Holy God," Angel said exasperated as they started walking again. "This money thing is generating monsters on this planet."

"Too early Angel. If you are calling them monsters for this, you have heard nothing yet," Rishabh continued further. "Once these drugged kids get old enough to walk and talk, they jump from lap to traffic signals and start singing the begging tunes."

Few workers were perspiring to clear the chocked sewage line. Angel saw them and bought some Vadapav (Indian burger) and water bottles.

"Come on guys take off your gloves, wash your hands. Let's have some rocking food together." Angel played music on Rishabh's iPhone and distributed the food with an essential ingredient of love. They all had curvy perspiration laced smiles which Nat Geo photographers click and get awards.

"But why are these kids not allowed to eat food outside," Angel asked as they kept on walking after having delicious Vadapav.

"Their diet is controlled. They cannot intake fats at all. They are supposed to look poor and haggard. Their body mass index is maintained below 15. The food prepared for them is pathetic. They are given liquid food with minimum nutrition value. Everything is monitored and regulated properly by these so called managers. They also undergo a training which includes counting, convincing, selling, where they learn to sell emotions. Some people are kept for recruiting new kids. They go to slums, find underprivileged, abandoned, orphan kids and become their parents. Every day the top performer is treated as a celebrity and given gifts. Incentives and bonuses on performances are also in place. They generate a highly competitive environment. And the worst of them all is their hate classes where they are made to cry and hate everyone who is not like them. That is why Krishna was saying they are tough kids but your kindness overpowered the hate in Krishna."

"Motherfucking managers. This is gross," Angel said, infuriated.

An old guy was trying to place a luggage inside a car. Rishabh quickly ran to help him. A smiling old face looked beautiful. "Thank you son," he said.

"This organized crime doesn't end here," Rishabh kept walking and talking. "Once these kids enter into adulthood, girls are dragged into prostitution and boys become pickpockets. Those who have leadership skills become local goons and then gradually enter into a bigger criminal world, also known as underworld. These underworld people are hardcore businessmen. They have organized every crime in a professional manner. Even if you want to arrange some good facilities for someone in jail you will be routed through underworld, such strong is their network. Begging is just one of their many businesses. They catch the young kids, train them and nurture them. They create such a support system for them that they cannot think of anything else. That is why despite of so much efforts from the government and NGOs, the number of beggars in our country keep on increasing rather than decreasing. I am sure there must be a franchisee system also for every signal."

"But there must be some genuine beggars too."

"Yes, very few I guess but it doesn't make any difference. They become a part of the system down the line. It's like saying there must be some genuine naxalites who fight against corrupt government officials. The purpose is long gone. It has become a business now."

"But when you can find all these dark secrets of begging business in such a short duration, there must be some authority in our country who knows about it. Why aren't they doing something about it?"

"I think the things have really gone out of control now. The business has spread to such an extent that everyone needs a share out of it and no one wants to stop it."

"But at least we can make people aware about the situation and make them stop donating to this begging business."

"That's the saddest part. Articles have been written, movies have been made, but we still buy their emotions. We run so hard in our lives that we don't spare a minute to hear the loud cries in our vicinity. It's because of this easily available support system of begging business that children like Krishna are devoid of their basic right to education. And we the so-called educated people easily fall prey to this begging business. The whole black money generated out of it is in few thousand crores which is funded for bigger crimes. The money I gave to Krishna yesterday might have funded someone's grave."

"What's the plan Rishabh? I am sure you must not have

worked so hard just to tell me this."

"Go slow sweetheart. I cannot handle so much of beauty with brains."

"Stop flirting, start blurting"

"It's a huge network, we cannot reach all of them. Let's first break a small link called Jaggu bhaiya. If we get successful, we can create a system of duplication through which other links can be broken too, thus disarming the whole network. But to create a system of duplication we will have to transform Jaggu from a bad guy to a good guy. We can also take help of media, NGOs and police to break the network but that will give only temporary solution. One breaking news, and they all will go into hibernation and after some time they will become active again once the media gets some other hot story to cover and I am sure where there is so much of money involved some legal power is also involved. Also, this solution is not duplicable. Your and my life alone is very short to cure this deep rooted problem. We need a system which can work on itself whether you and I are present or not. We will have to get inside to break them from within. And that can happen only with a change of mindset. First, we will have to work on Jaggu's mindset. We will have to make him realize that what he is doing is wrong. For that we will have to incept few thoughts in his head through some chicanery. Once he is filled with enough of guilt, we will propel him towards expiation. Once this person is ready with a mindset, he will push other managers also to do exactly the same what he did, obviously with proper training and support. This will weaken the whole network of crime factory."

They were sitting on a bench by now. "That gave me a

near orgasmic feeling Mr. Nolan (Hollywood director) but don't you think this inception solution sounds too good to be true."

"Any new idea which challenges the prevailing mindset, which includes a paradigm shift, sounds too good to be true. When Steve Jobs said he doesn't want a keypad in his cell phone, people said the same thing. When Ratan Tata unveiled his thought of making a car of rupees one lakh, people said the same thing. When Dhirubhai Ambani said he wants a call rate at a price of a postal letter, people said the same thing. I know transforming Jaggu bhaiya will involve a lot of brainstorming, micro level planning, great team work, risk assessment, rigorous management, and smooth execution but the day we will see those kids in a school and not at traffic signal, everything, every effort will be worth it. And one day this too good to be true idea will not remain an idea anymore; it will become a way of life. Jaggu bhaiya transforming other Jaggu bhaiya will become a process.

"You seem to be a master of transformation. You just transformed me into a horny one. Now before I corrupt your mind and you start asking for feast again, please tell me how are we exactly going to work on this Jaggu bhaiya's mindset?"

"We will have to track his daily routine first."

"How?"

"We will have to find someone who can spy on him and give some more details than my transmitter on his jacket."

"I got a guy. He can help us."

They reached Sandywich, a small sandwich stall. The smaller lanes of Ahmedabad have so much to explore especially the luscious food for the foodaholics. Sandywich was no different but the USP of this place was the guy called

Sandy.

He was an artist. He was making everything dance, the breads, the knife, the sauces, the stuffing while preparing the sandwiches. His hands moved smoothly from here to there like a belly of a belly dancer. Watching him preparing the sandwich was a treat to eyes but ears received a far better treat than eyes, his constant blabbering.

"Yo brother from another mother, how do you want your mouth to be exploded today?" he asked a customer with his American accent.

"With a schezwan," said a loyal customer.

"Today you are going to have the best sandwich of your life buddy. This is Sandy's schezwan, I bet you can't have just one."

Now whatever he said, he started composing a music with a knife and tapping his fingers on table, along with preparing the sandwich too.

"I am telling you man, life is a bitch
You gotta eat Sandy's sandwich
Be it yo wife, yo galfan or yo bombastic boss
There is always gonna be some kich kich
But you have to be on the pitch
So you gotta eat Sandy's Sandwich

Bro I know yo ass is torn, you need a stitch
Chacko, please hand over some cheese out of the fridge
What I was saying, there is always an emergency switch
Yes you are right, its Sandy's sandwich

Let me tell now the secret of ingredients so rich
There is love my friend connected through a bridge

Keep spreading the love dude, never ditch
Here's your Sandy's Schezwan sandwich"

He handed over the delicious looking sandwich to the customer.

"I love you Sandy. Be my boyfriend," a girl standing in a queue shouted to him. He was quite popular in past few weeks.

"Love you too lady. Keep spreading the love but you got a little late as I am already committed to this wonderful mate," he showed the sandwich and handed over to the next customer.

Angel waived at Sandy from distance. Watching her he instantly announced, "Guys and girls I am signing off, my buddy Chacko will take over from here" and a guy in jumpsuit wearing some heavy metal round his neck, an inverted cap on his head comes in.

"Cool wrist band bro," Sandy said to a guy, looking at his hand while walking. "Nice hairdo lady," he said to another girl and everyone was smiling and waving at him. He was a little celebrity near that Sandywich stall.

"How are you gurumaiya (the teacher)?" he greeted Angel.

"Gurumaiya found a boyfriend finally. Meet Rishabh," Angel exulted.

Sandy's eyes went bigger looking at Rishabh and he made a second announcement, "Fifty percent discount on sandwiches guys. It's party time" and the whole crowd mostly students went hoopla over the announcement while some of them hugged him and gave him an air flight with their hands.

"Are you on a mission to spread madness on our planet?" Rishabh asked Angel.

She smiled and replied "At least it's better than pretention of maturity"

After settling down, Sandy arranged three chairs and brought cold drinks.

"I must say Sandy, what you were doing there is a shear talent. You are an artist," Rishabh exclaimed.

"Oh no bhaiya, what you just saw, everything is a creation of Angel di. I was a petty pickpocket just a year back until I collided with this nuclear," he said pointing at Angel. "I still remember that fortunate day when I stole her.."

He was interrupted by Angel, "We need your help Sandy"

"Yes, but before that I want to hear the story," Rishabh interjected back.

"There is no story Rishabh," Angel raised her eyebrows in frustration. "Sandy was on a different way. I showed him my way. He liked it and started walking it. That's it."

"She is being modest bhaiya. She has completely changed my life."

"Oh come on," she got up annoyed. "Go on morons. Waste your time flattering yourself. Call me once you are done" and she left them and her story.

"Yes Sandy, I am all ears," Rishabh said as he watched Angel play with a canine.

"Pickpocketing is an art and I was the master of it, one of the best. It involves a high level of glibness, right from identifying the prey to making it lighter."

Rishabh chortled at his selection of words.

"You need a cat's stealth, a cheetah's speed and a fox's brain to accomplish every theft. It's like hunting and my hunting grounds were Kalupur, Vastrapur, Law garden, Manek chowk, Navratri clubs and the best and biggest of them all, music concerts. I was always the first one to buy the ticket of Arijit Singh's concert in Ahmedabad. There always were two artists performing in the concert but people could see only the one who was under the lights. While Arijit touched their soul, I put a hole in their pockets. I used to keep moving, untraceable and uncatchable."

"May be that's why you have a penchant for food and music. I mean based on the selection of your hunting grounds."

"I had no doubt about it but I must say that you are a perfect match for Angel di. You are really sharp."

Rishabh smiled. "So how did you meet the nuclear?"

"I was on a theft spree in a vegetable market when I saw an old lady with a visible purse inside her bag. My eyes always fell on oldies and fatties so that I could easily outrun them in case there was a chase and this lady did not even know when I drilled her bag. No chase, no commotion, I was so glib. The farther the thieves from lenses, be it eyes' or cameras', the longer and brighter their career but that day destiny itself shifted its whole focus on me. I was under lights and camera. I felt like someone was stalking me. In theft business, we had to keep running. Stopping meant either a jail or a beating of an illegal thief by legal thieves, the maddening crowd. I kept running but when the stalker is Angel di, you have to show your athletic skills at the very best. She never takes no for an answer. She kept chasing me like a ghost, on the roads, lanes, streets, bus stand, everywhere and the thought of why is she not shouting, to gather the crowd, frightened me even more. The chase continued for almost thirty minutes after which I finally surrendered. I turned around, went towards her on a skywalk and vomited my scripted lines.

"Please take this purse. I will never do this again, I am really sorry. Please leave me."

"I don't need this purse," Angel di said. *"It's your hard earned money. Gudiya needs you, please come with me."*

"Gudiya suffers from polio but she is a very smart kid. She lives in the neighborhood. Her father used to work in a steel plant near Sanand who died in an accident. That day her innocent words even made me cry.

"Sandesh bhaiya, my father works very hard in a factory. He is very tired that's why asleep. Why is everybody crying so much?"

And then one day she met Angel di who taught her '*I love you*' and she came running towards me that day, shouting '*I love you Sandesh bhaiya, I love you Sandesh bhaiya*'.

Rishabh looked at Angel with moist eyes. She was giving a high five to a ragamuffin.

"Gudiya needs you was enough for me to run towards her house. When we reached there she was lying on bed, a doctor and a nurse besides her. Doctor said she had a very high temperature and she needs to be hospitalized immediately. Since Gudiya was adamant to not to go to the hospital, Angel di had arranged a doctor for her."

"Why are you not going to the hospital Gudiya," Sandy asked.

"I will go," she said slowly with a heavy, forceful voice, *"but only if you promise me one thing"*

"What is it? I can do anything for you."

"I want you to quit pickpocketing. I want you to live a good life."

Sandy went quiet for a moment. Angel placed a hand on his shoulder and gave a nod.

"Alright, but let's go to the hospital first. Let's go," Sandy said and

carried her in his arms.

"After that Angel di taught me everything, from speaking English, to making sandwiches to acquiring customers for a business. Gudiya loves her a lot. They always make some sort of symbol with horizontal and vertical hand and then smile at each other but they never tell me what it is."

Rishabh smirked as if he knew what it was.

"Are you guys done with your bromantic stories? Shall we discuss some work now?" Angel said, coming and sitting on a chair.

"Yes di, what is it? Please tell me," Sandy replied.

"We want to know about Jaggu bhaiya, his past, his present, his daily activities, every available detail of him"

"Is he the one who manages kids at traffic signal?"

"Correct," Rishabh said.

"All I know about him is, he is a sadist, an alcoholic who beats children at his will. He works under Baba who has a lot of faith in him. That's it. That's all I know for now. Rest I will find out tomorrow, every detail. I know how to get it. Don't worry Angel di, job will be done. Chacko bring two sandwiches here please," Sandy shouted to the rapper looking guy.

****

Porsche stopped at a distance from Angel's bungalow in sector 22.

"So you and Gudiya fabricated a story to transform Sandesh to Sandy?" Rishabh said.

"What the...? How did you..?" Angel's vocab was robbed.

"I know it. And that's why you and Gudiya make a T symbol for the top secret every time you meet."

"So Sandy knows it?" she asked, surprised.

"No he does not. I just worked it out from what he said. You would have never left Gudiya alone and chased Sandy for almost thirty minutes if she was so ill."

After that, no words were exchanged but they communicated a lot in silence with a constant smile. Words are more like wireless communication while touch is a wired one and more effective. Touch is the first language of communication we learn right after birth. That's why the babies hold everything tight in their small palms. They want to communicate with touch. She expressed her feelings with that first language. She held his hands and kissed his palms. She gently rummaged his hair and then stroked his cheeks. He leaned forward and kissed her forehead holding her face from behind her neck. She hugged him and gave a peck on his cheeks. Rishabh caressed her back and rubbed his cheeks with hers. He kissed her neckline, placed her hair aside and kissed her back. With eyes closed they hugged each other softly communicating their feelings strongly. They made out their feelings inside that black beauty. Nelson stood above the Porsche like a Superdog.

7

The university road of Ahmedabad is inundated with positive vibes all the time. The colleges spread around the university keep abundant flow of knowledge. Youngsters, mostly students, talk about dreams, girls, boys, friendship, games, sports, etc. Likes of Ruthraj, feeding high appetite students with maskaban and tea, and numerous love stories blossoming in campuses make it a vibrant place of Ahmedabad.

"You have already transformed Sandy," Rishabh said as they walked on the university road. "Sandy is helping us to transform Jaggu. The system is already in place, Angel. What I was thinking, you have already done it."

"There was nothing to transform in Sandy. He was already a good person. He just needed a direction. Jaggu is a different case, he is a cunt, a pussy, he beats children."

"You start cursing him every time you hear his name and that really motivates me and keeps me focused. So keep cursing."

Angel saw a handicapped guy without a leg, sitting beside the boundary wall of CEPT University.

"You want to eat something?" Angel asked him.

The guy joined hands and nodded with tears in his eyes. She held his hands and wiped off his tears. She quickly ran towards a maskaban stall, bought two of them and a tea.

"Have it. It's delicious," she gave it to him.

Rishabh on the other hand found a barber nearby who had arranged his set up on a boundary wall with a chair and a mirror. The poor guy gained some energy and lost a heavy beard resulting in a classy look and a satiated smile.

"Thank you daughter," he said. "You are a God's angel for me. I was very hungry. And you made me look younger, son," he chuckled. "Thank you, both of you. May the Almighty fulfill all your wishes."

"Here, that's for you," another person came up with some oranges and a water bottle. He gave it to the poor man. He just placed his stall of oranges nearby.

"Oh! Thank you so much," Angel said and tried to give him some money but he refused.

"Angel, you help so many people. How do you manage the finance part? Do you ask from your dad or you have some source of income?" Rishabh asked out of curiosity.

"I never ask my Dad."

"I thought so but hey, what your Dad does? How come we haven't talked about our families yet?"

"We will talk about it later. Right now do you want to know how do I earn money?"

"I somehow have an idea after Rehmaan Chacha's painting incident and Sandy's business development with your help, but your crazy methods are always a refresher. So yes, I want to know more than a Victoria's secret. Go ahead, whole Ahmedabad is your playground."

"Bhaiya," she called oranges' guy.

"Yes madam"

"Do you want to sell all these oranges within an hour?"

"That's impossible. It has never happened in my fifteen years of experience."

"I just love the word impossible. Ok listen, if we sell it within an hour, you will have to share fifty percent of your profit.

"Deal, but don't forget within an hour part".

She gave the thumbs up.

"Uncle," she asked the poor guy. "Can you do something, anything, any talent, any hobby you have?"

"I can play this flute," he said taking out a flute from inside his shawl.

"Amazing, keep playing it." She then turned towards Rishabh. "Rishabh bring your Porsche, take some oranges, sit on the bonnet and start juggling"

Rishabh looked at her with squinted eyes.

"You will learn it, don't worry. Start doing it. Come on, we don't have enough time. Go fast," she said snapping her fingers.

Rishabh took some oranges and started walking towards Porsche, juggling. He was a quick learner.

"Bhaiya keep bags of dozen oranges ready," she said to the oranges' guy. "Let the show begin."

And then she started selling oranges to each and every one in her ten meter radius. Those oranges became the remedy to every problem of the world. She would have sold oranges to Mr. Trump saying they could help fight terrorism. She sold it to fat people, to lanky fellows, to guys without girlfriends, to guys with girlfriends having low libido, to geniuses, to dumbos, to uncles, to aunties, while the flute and

Rishabh juggling on a Porsche helped in pulling the crowd. Meanwhile two guys showed some indecency towards Angel.

"Mam your oranges are really nice and big" and they felt their necks almost crunched under the muscled arms of Rishabh.

"Give them five dozens each as a penalty for misbehavior, Rishabh"

Within fifty minutes the whole stall was empty, leaving the owner of the stall scratching his head. She earned six hundred bucks within an hour out of which she gave five hundred to that poor guy.

"Catch it," she threw an orange towards Sandy as she saw him coming while continuing walking with Rishabh.

"I caught everything di," he said catching an orange. "Jaggu was a commerce graduate who used to work as an accountant in Kalupur market. In his part time he used to practice photography and talk to strangers, a very happy soul he was. He used to talk a lot with everyone, a very likeable personality but that day in 2002 riots, he lost his everything. His whole family was killed. His father was burned alive. His mother and sister were raped and then locked inside their burning house. He had gone outside Ahmedabad for work before riots occurred. When he came back, his whole world was vanished, he was devastated completely."

Rishabh and Angel froze after hearing Sandy's words. The same Jaggu to whom Angel was cursing some time back had now gained sympathy of both.

"Years of pain has made him the way he is today," Sandy continued. "Nothing affects him now. He is indifferent to situations, his emotions are gone and alcohol substantiates the numbness. His morning starts with alcohol and then he checks the weight of the kids. If any kid is found more than the desired weight, he starts beating that kid. He then delegates the work to kids, ladies and oldies. Then he checks with the food department handled by Lala. He has a device which tells the nutritional value of the food. After that, he goes to the top floor of a building from where he keeps an eye on his people. In the evening another person comes in and he leaves to meet Baba. Baba handles the whole begging business of Gujarat. He generates bags full of money out of begging every day. He handles a lot of them like Jaggu but Jaggu is his favorite. It is said Baba gave shelter to Jaggu after those riots. Everyday Jaggu goes to a Temple and a Mosque but never goes inside. He just stands outside for some time and then leaves. Every night he visits a prostitute named Laila but before that, he arranges a training session for kids where they are taught to hate everyone unlike them apart from basic mathematics and other required skills for begging. They teach them everything specially before sleeping so that during sleep their brain can retain most of the information."

Angel and Rishabh sighed when Sandy was done telling them whatever information he had collected.

"Angel di, I know you always want to help the destitute people but this one is too messy. Please do not get into this, this is really dangerous. There are many people out there who care about you. For their sake, not this time, please di."

"But Sandy what's wrong is wrong, it has to be stopped. Someone will have to take a step."

"Not you Angel di, we shall inform police. You please don't get into this."

"No," Rishabh interrupted firmly. "Informing police will not be a solution. Police will destroy Jaggu, Baba will create another. This will never end. Creators always have an upper hand over destructors. We need to think of an alternative. Don't worry, I think I got a plan and trust me nothing will happen to anyone."

Angel and Sandy kept staring at Rishabh with a big question mark on their faces.

"Let's get caffeinated first," Rishabh said.

****

"Your three Crangel Café Sir," waiter placed the order on the table.

"Baba is creating bad Jaggus by taking advantage of their bad situations," Rishabh started unveiling his plan. "We will create good Jaggus by providing them good situations. I know it's like taking meat out of Lion's mouth, but the good news is Jaggu has the tendency to transform. Baba had already transformed him once post riots, so there are high chances that he will transform again. People's transformation happen through situations not through people, it's psychological. By creating certain situations in Jaggu's life we can transform him again, only this time, for good. Something as intense as riots leave a profound impact on a person's mindset, the whole upbringing, the whole value system is vanquished. You are not able to differentiate between right and wrong. Even after twelve years, riots are still on inside his mind. Changing the mindset of such a person is a mammoth task. We will have to create positive situations as impactful as riots, not just once multiple times. If we constantly hammer the positive things in his mind for 21 days, science says we get good results. Once Jaggu's mindset is changed, we will just have to give him a direction. Now all we need is those situations where Jaggu is forced to discern his life, pre and post riots from a different angle."

"Powerful, impactful, positive situations?" Angel asked in question.

"As intense as riots?" Sandy corroborated.

"Mass celebration of festivals show a lot of positivity," Angel said.

"In riots they use weapons. We can use flowers, balloons, decorative to intensify the emotions while involving him in such celebrations. We can make him dance also." Sandy added.

Rishabh shook his head. "No, this will not work. He must have seen all this in past twelve years. We need to grab his attention towards those small little things which are more powerful and impactful than any weapon of the world. When do you get more emotional, while lighting a cracker during a celebration or watching a baby laugh uncontrollably?" Rishabh elucidated. "We need to fill the abyss of Jaggu's current life with these small little things with big impact. Now such things can only be found from his past life about which we still do not know much. So to understand him more, I need to meet Laila, the only person he meets off the duty, where he must be sharing some of his left over emotions. And since he keeps his jacket away during that meeting, I cannot hear the conversation properly. So I will have to meet her in person somehow."

Sandy gave a confused look but Angel's flaring eyes made Rishabh add, "Obviously with your consent sweetheart."

"On a condition," Angel snapped instantly.

"What condition?"

Angel turned towards Sandy with furious looks.

"Oh yeah, my sandwiches are calling me," he said and left in no time.

Angel without saying a word kept looking at Rishabh, no movement, just her wide opened eyes penetrating Rishabh's. He was totally confused on what the condition could be and Angel's silence created havoc inside his brain.

"Will you please speak?" Rishabh said.

"I want to see it," she mumbled instantly.

"What?"

"I want to see it," she said loud and clear.

"But what?"

"I WANT," she said gesturing her hand towards him, "TO SEE IT, your body. Before that Laila watches anything, I want to see everything."

Excitement, embarrassment, confusion; mixed feelings are like Chinese bhel (Indian dish) and Rishabh's top pot was overflowing with it.

"You mean the whole package?" Rishabh asked.

"Yes the whole package," Angel clarified.

"But Angel, don't worry. It will be a no show, no blow thing with Laila. I am going there just to gather some information. Please try to understand."

"I don't know that. I just want to see the package, that's it."

"What if I say I haven't shaved?"

"What if I shout in front of everyone that my boyfriend here doesn't shave his balls off ?"

Rishabh made a pitiful face, "Please don't do that" He looked here and there for a while and then said, "You know it would be really embarrassing. I will feel like being punished."

"What will be embarrassing? My shouting here or you showing me the package?"

"Both of course," he retorted. "Sweetheart why are you doing this to me? I love you," he made a forlorn attempt.

"Hello young lady," Angel turned to the nearby table. "What will you do if your boyfriend tells you that he is going to visit an escort service tonight?"

"I will chop off his balls," the girl replied.

"Thank you" Angel said and turned back to Rishabh, "Still a decent punishment I guess."

"Ruthless," he murmured.

****

Porsche stopped at a distance from her bungalow in sector 22 of Gandhinagar.

"Jump on backseat Mr. Performer," Angel said.

Rishabh went onto the back seat while Angel pressed the convert button to enjoy the show.

"Let the curtain rise and show begin," Angel said rubbing her hands.

Rishabh smiled and started unbuttoning his shirt, his chiseled body gradually becoming more and more visible out of that black shirt. Rishabh put his shirt aside.

"Holy cuts," Angel said. "Why do you hide it all the time?"

"Alright, so you are happy," Rishabh said. "The purpose is solved. Show over."

"Oh no no no. The show has just begun my love. Let's now unveil the very first gadget of mankind."

"Someone please help me. I want to go home," Rishabh cried like a baby.

Angel laughed at that. "That was really cute, now please start the show and please my eyes sweetheart."

"Ruthless," Rishabh murmured. He slowly opened his belt strap with trembling hands and started unzipping his pants.

"Stop," Angel said and climbed over her seat towards Rishabh. She landed a passionate kiss on his lips. Her hands started moving on his bare chest. It was their longest kiss till now. Rishabh slid his hands inside her top, caressing and feeling the residence of a beautiful soul. She then placed her face on his broad chest. "Listen, take care of yourself," she said. "It's a dangerous place where you are going."

"Don't worry. I will be alright."

"And by the way you just took the flavor of the feast. How was it?"

"It looks lasciviously luscious."

"But it's not yet ready," she said, opened the door in split second and ran away taking his shirt slipping it inside her top.

Rishabh watched her from the back seat with a bare chest smiling at her vivaciousness.

8

Laila was Jamnaben's girl. Since Ahmedabad does not have any specific red light area like Kolkata or Mumbai, Jamnaben had to keep shifting her brothel. Sandy told Rishabh about the auto drivers who could get him to Laila. That night Rishabh chewed the beetle nut, changed his hairstyle, wore a printed yellow shirt over brown pants and adopted a gait which made him look like a jerk. He moved towards an auto with a number plate 6969. The driver was listening to a *baby doll* song pictured on Sunny Leone. It was the only auto parked in a narrow alley nearby Ashram road at 11:30pm. He grabbed the accessory of an auto, spit red on road and lowered his face towards the driver.

"Where to?" driver asked.

"Badnaam gali," Rishabh said showing his red stained teeth, holding the beetle in his mouth from falling inside an auto thereby sounding like a celebrity politician of Bihar.

Driver smiled and gestured to sit. The auto in no time reached the dark and narrow lanes with foul smell. Rishabh wondered about self-unawareness of such places in Ahmedabad. Jaggu's visiting hours to Laila were 10 to 12. So Rishabh chose to reach there just before 12. Auto stopped near a half-constructed building. Two heavily built guys were smoking cigarettes at the entrance gate.

"Come on. Follow me. Let me take you to the wonderland," driver said, his body language talking obsequiousness.

A guy in a formal shirt, khaki pants and black shoes with two bundles of notes walked past Rishabh.

"Jamnaben, how are you doing?" driver asked to a forty something woman in a green sari chewing beetle nut sitting on a bed placed outside that building.

"Not so good Ratan. You already know how Amdavadis duped their money in real estate. The builder of this building has no money to construct it further. He is not getting any investor so he rented me the place. It looks like recession has hit our field also. I don't know what these motherfucking wives of Ahmedabad have started doing to their husbands; no one is coming these days. And there are so much of exams nowadays, poor youngsters have no time for sex. This bloody internet also has affected our business. The boys and girls are casually talking about sex, they do not need us anymore and you know how Ahmedabad market is? We have to keep moving and still I have to pay these bastards regularly. Even surviving has become a challenge now."

"Don't worry Jamnaben. Good days will come, have faith. By the way here is your customer," he said gesturing towards Rishabh.

"Oh great, Please have a seat," Jamnaben said to Rishabh.

"Thank you Jamnaben," Rishabh said sitting on that stained bed.

"How much time do you want to spend son?" she enquired.

"Actually Jamnaben I have a problem" Rishabh started throwing his emotional bait. "And I think only you can understand and solve my problem."

"Of course, that's the actual service we provide; lighten the emotional baggage of our customers. Sex helps quicken the process."

"I used to love a girl madly. We spent some memorable time together. I used to love her like a *Majnu* and could give away my life for her, but that betrayer married someone else yesterday" Rishabh said with tearful eyes. "I fucking hate her. But this *Majnu* wants a *Laila* today, Please Jamnaben, please give me my *Laila*. I will never forget this favor of yours. Please give me my *Laila*." Rishabh started playing the psychological game now.

Jamnaben tried to console the phony *Majnu*, "Don't worry son, I have a Laila for you. She is the perfect answer to your problem. Trust me, you will have the most wonderful night tonight." She turned towards the entrance gate, "Jumbo," she called one of the guys. "Take this gentleman to room number 8 and tell Jaggu to leave the room."

Rishabh's internals celebrated for the successful landing. He deposited one thousand bucks with Jamnaben and followed Jumbo. Jumbo's frame was bigger than Rishabh. He wore cargo pants and black t-shirt. There was no lift in the building. In the dim-lit lobby of the first floor there was an African guy in knickers smoking weed. Few walls were yet to be plastered. They were painted red by tobacco spitting. They reached outside room no. 8 on second floor. Normal people usually knock but Jumbos bang the doors.

"Who is that motherfucker?" Jaggu shouted from inside.

"Time's up. Please come out," Jumbo replied calmly.

Moments later a big frame in a brown jacket, white vest and black denims equivalent to Jumbo came out of the room. Soaked in alcohol, he started staring at both of them from head to toe. The red lit background of the room along with red eyes of Jaggu made the place eerie.

"Let's go Jaggubhai. You have a lot of work in the morning," Jumbo said politely taking him away while signaling Rishabh to go inside the room.

"You will sleep with Laila I will make you sleep permanently, motherfucker," Jaggu said walking and talking under the influence of alcohol holding the shoulder of the Jumbo.

Rishabh went inside, shut the door and started abusing at the door, "I will kill you motherfucker, I will butcher your balls thereby killing your unborn kids. I will shove an Eiffel tower up your ass and barbeque you to death. I will…"

"Hold on gentleman," A seductive voice from behind told Rishabh.

She came out from the bathroom in white shorts, placed her one foot on bed, one on ground showing her soft and creamy legs. The tight unbuttoned chequered red shirt tied at belly button was a clear boner. Voluptuous would be a tiny word to describe her. Even her sweat beads would have to run a marathon over her curves. She could break the pointers of machines indicating testosterone levels of guys in front of her.

"You seem to be very angry. I love angry young guys and I want you to preserve your anger for a while so that you can vent it here on me not on the door. Come here gentleman, make me angry too and do not shout on that poor guy. He is already disturbed a lot."

That last statement from Laila was like a free access to National Data Center.

"Really, what happened to that scumbag?"

"Doesn't matter dear, you are here to get the pleasure not to hear the painful stories. Come here, let's make you bigger."

Even with free access to data center you need to seduce few officials to get the exact piece of information without planting the seed of doubt in their minds. Rishabh went on to seduce the seductive. The room literally had nothing in it except a bed and a chair. He walked towards her, ditching her lips he blew air inside her ear. The resulting moan from the master Laila could have relieved any virgin but Rishabh had mastered his self-control. She held his hand and hugged him tight. She started kissing him and unbuttoning his shirt.

"Stop," Rishabh said pushing her lips away.

"What happened?"

"I think I am not going to get bigger today."

She touched his groin and said, "Oh God, what happened? That's rude actually. I feel insulted."

"No little man can escape your beauty without saluting you. It's actually my fault. My girlfriend married to someone else yesterday so to release the stress, I self-abused quite a lot of times. I am sorry."

She started laughing aloud. Rishabh had to hold her and make her sit from falling on ground laughing so hard. He sat on a chair with unbuttoned shirt and rested his feet on bed. He kept smiling at her honest laugh. It looked like she had an honest hearty laugh after a long time.

"So what now?" she asked after getting stabilized. "You want to try once again? May be we can get the little man come out of the hangover?"

"Not possible. This hangover is going to last longer."

"Listen, you have already paid and I am here to serve you. Whatever you say, I am ready for it."

"How about changing the roles? Let me serve you tonight, beautiful lady."

"Well in that case, little man can take rest but only a set of powerful hands can take up the job."

"You are forgetting the power of a tongue your highness."

"No way, Cunnilingus on me is bad for you. I am not going to let you do it."

"I am not going to touch you," Rishabh expounded. "I will just talk," he added.

She smiled with squinted eyes. "You are mad," she said.

"I am serious. I can give you an orgasm with my words."

"I would love to have one then."

"Among all the nature's gifts, which one is your favorite?"

"Rain, I just love it."

"Alright, please close your eyes and listen to what I am saying"

She smiled at his strange request but acquiesced to it.

"Imagine you are walking on a lonely highway amongst the mountains breathing the fresh air". She started taking a deep breath.

"No fear, no doubt, no insecurities, no confusion, it's just you and the nature in their best moods. Keep walking and take in the fresh air." With her smile meter on, she took another deep breath.

"Keep smiling because the clouds are done wrapping up the gifts for you. It's time now for showering them onto you.

Don't miss that sheep grazing on the mountain." She looked radiant now.

"Clouds welcome you with a thunderous applause and with open hands you are ready to embrace your love. The very first drop of rain plants a kiss on your forehead. Your heart beats faster pumping more blood thereby inducing an adrenalin rush. You start moaning as the drop moves from your forehead to your cheeks. The next drop falls on your hand, slowly moving onto your fingers. You tighten your fist making yourself ready to be drenched in love. Another one falls on your petal like lips. You touch it with your tongue, taste it and sip it. The shiver runs in your body as you feel more of them. You have no control. The wind embraces your body, taking you out of control. With that tight embrace, you are now totally wet."

"Yes I am. Keep going"

"You feel few of the drops running down from your chin to your neckline to your breast making you clench your fist tighter. They land on your belly giving you a tickling sensation". She started moaning again.

"They kiss you everywhere, to your forehead, your eyes, your cheeks, your back, your lips, your shoulders, your neck, your breasts, your belly, your thighs and your soul. You start shivering and getting out of control". She starts moaning heavily as Rishabh slowly sprinkles his love inducing words into her ears.

"Few of those drops travel more to pass through the gates and get inside your pleasure hall where you have gathered enough of explosives ready to explode. As they touch the most delicate, the most sensitive part of your body, you explode with excitement. You clench your fist tighter,"

94

she started breathing heavily now. Rishabh's mesmerizing voice was doing wonders for her.

"The urge of getting more gives you more and more and more. Each drop gets warm in there and explodes the splashes of excitement. The series of such explosions give you a blissful feeling of being in heaven. With each release and contraction you are.."

She suddenly outburst a sigh after oozing out her unrestrained emotions inside her white shorts. With eyes closed she moved her hand towards Rishabh. He held it with both his hands.

"What did you just do? I have never experienced such a thing in my life," she said, eyes still closed.

"Did I serve you well?"

"You just blew away my senses, sweetheart", she said opening her eyes now.

Rishabh smiled and did not say anything for long. She sat in silence with a smile of huge satisfaction pondering over the whole new experience of verbal orgasm.

"What?" she asked smiling. "Why are you not saying anything?"

"You beauty has outsized my vocabulary"

"You are different," she said.

"No, I am jealous actually."

"Of whom?"

"That scumbag. Why do you have a soft corner for him?"

"Who? Jaggu?"

"See. Even his name rhymes with shit."

"Oh, please don't say that. Poor guy is a victim of riots. He deserves a better life."

"What had happened with him?" Rishabh hunched

forward, his tone, his eye contact, his posture, everything was highly convincing to make Laila speak.

"Do you have a family?" she asked.

"Yes I do."

"What if they all just disappear all of a sudden?" Rishabh knew what she was talking about. He did not interrupt, just listened.

"Family is everything. It's the root to hold you strong during your tough times. Family brews love, the most essential fuel to move this world. It has an amazing power of healing almost everything instantly. Good families form great society. To have a family is a blessing from Almighty but people like Jaggu and I are devoid of this blessing. I am an orphan since birth. So my fate from begging to prostitution was decided and I did not have tough time to accept it because I was prepared, but Jaggu," she sighed. "They tore his life apart. No warnings, just a blind fold rip off. Yesterday you had a beautiful family, today you don't. Who gave you the right to destroy someone's family like that? His father was a tailor who loved cricket. Whenever India defeated Pakistan, he used to fire crackers and dance with kids. That day those bastards were dancing when his father was burning. Jaggu says his mother was the best cook in this world. Every day after work the welcome smell of food from kitchen would make him run towards her mother and hug her. That day she packed him his favorite, Chicken Biryani, the last one he had, made by her hands. His younger sister was a movie buff and she had a huge crush on Hrithik Roshan. He could not resist sharing all his secrets with her and she being the naughty sister, would blackmail him for gifts. Jaggu bought imported cosmetics for her not knowing that dead bodies do not accept gifts. I have seen him cry not for days but for years. Every day he goes to the temple and the mosque just to ask this question, "What was their fault?" She was in tears. Rishabh found himself crying too.

9

"Jaggu needs a family," Rishabh said to Angel in Seva café while dishwashing along with her. Other volunteers were taking orders and cooking the food. "I used to think that Baba has created Jaggu but we only have created both of them somehow, for our greed of power and money. Jaggu is in trauma from past twelve years and there is no one to take care of him. Such a person handling those kids is a total chaos in the society. It's a hypocrisy. First we tarnish their family which is a linchpin to form a society and then blame them for ruining the society. This whole world indeed is a family Angel and there are many like Jaggu who unfortunately have been excluded from the family. The only way to change his mindset is to get him back into the family."

The ambience of Seva café produced positive vibrations. No one worked for money over there, they worked for love. There were no customers, only guests, no waiters or cooks, only volunteers. Volunteers danced with guests, had a good chat with them, everybody had fun. No one expected money from guests. All bills were made of zero rupees. If any money came in from guests, it was used for next day's preparations.

The entire café had quotes on good life and spreading love, on its walls.

"Alright, so we need to introduce some new people in his life who will become his family," Angel suggested.

"Exactly"

"But how do we do that? He doesn't meet anyone?"

"You know when grownups do not meet people whom they are supposed to meet or do not visit places which they must visit, you give them sedatives and when they wake up they should ask.."

****

"Where am I?" Jaggu asked.

"Don't worry son, you are safe now," Rehman Chacha said. "You were lying unconscious on the road. Nobody was helping you. Anyhow my daughter Sharfun brought you here with the help of few others. How are you feeling now?"

The best thing about parallel positive world is people over there trust each other a lot. When Angel explained everything to Rehman Chacha, he instantly agreed to be a family to Jaggu without asking much questions. Rishabh on the other hand learned a technique over internet on how to sedate someone without his or her knowledge. He gave a colorless and odorless spray to Krishna which he sprayed on Jaggu's jacket. The spray was so effective that the whole event of unconsciousness could be well timed and planned with just the number of sprays. Jaggu fell unconscious exactly when he was on his way to temple and mosque.

Jaggu tried to get up from bed but fell on it again.

"Relax son, take rest. You are not well yet," Zubeda,

Rehnman Chacha's wife told Jaggu. Nafisa brought a glass of water for him. Jaggu drank some water and felt better.

"I should leave now," Jaggu said.

"Wait," Zubeda told him. "You must be hungry. Have some food first and then you can leave." The aroma of Chicken Biryani made tear glands active rather than saliva glands of Jaggu.

Rishabh and Angel were watching everything on a small display in Porsche through a small spy camera placed inside the home.

Meanwhile Rehman chacha put on the television and started surfing sports channels. He stopped on a repeat telecast of India Pakistan cricket match. Jaggu could not control the storm of emotions. The images of his mother, father and sister started revolving around his head which created a hurricane inside his brain. He started running out of that house. Rishabh and Angel saw him walking swiftly past them wiping off his tears. Angel gave a high five to Rishabh. "Few more sprays and Jaggu will get his family back."

"Hmm," Rishabh gave a reply in confusion.

"What happened?"

"Even though Jaggu gets his family back what will prompt him to leave his current profession and help those kids in moving to school"

"Simple. Another profession"

"Wow, you just gave me a boner"

"Shut up and tell me what profession will be good for him"

"I love your usage of antithesis," Rishabh flirting began, "And your hair and your eyes and your lips and your.."

"Photography"

"You know photography too. Wow I did not know that. Can you please picture us together?"

"The profession, Rishabh. Photography!" Angel exclaimed.

"Oh yes, the photography," Rishabh jumped up his seat.

"But who will help us to get him into photography. Do you know someone?"

"Yes I do and he is the best for this job," Rishabh said smiling at his own thoughts.

"Who?"

"Viren, my agent."

10

"Read, motherfuckers, read," Viren shouted in his office.

Just like Viren his whole office ambience also shouted like him. Coffee machine said, "Go back and dig the stack". Male urinals said, "Size matters, not of the one you are holding but of your paycheck, so go back and read". Female washroom shouted, "Focus on career. Lusty adulating boyfriends are for free, costly cosmetics are not. Go back and read." Sofas spread everywhere said, "Bang me while reading". Dustbins shouted, "Either read or get inside me". One of the walls said, "Those who can't read are illiterates, those who don't are FUCKING ILLITERATES." Another one said, "Welcome to the world of erection, arousals and intoxication, pick up a manuscript and get started." A white board said, "Take that marker and jizz it all over me with your thoughts"

"My warriors," Viren began his morning speech at the center of his office.

"We represent writers and they owe this world a lot," he began with a slow pace.

"Starting from Maharishi Valmiki and Vedvyas, all of them have given us the direction. Writers are our headlights on the dark highway of life. They preserve our past and foresee our future," he now increased his pace slowly.

"And we, right here at *Shyren* find the best of them so that our coming generations are enlightened with great writings. So my dear ferocious readers, we have a responsibility here and a great responsibility deserves great perks," he said and took time to look at everyone in the office.

"Look at that stack of pages in front of you. They contain hundreds of thousands of words but somewhere inside them are golden words, a bestseller and you know who gets the gold?," he asked and then answered it with a fading smile and powerful pitch, "The one who digs the most and I promise you the more you will dig here the more you will dig your beautiful and voluptuous wife in the lavish room of your 5BHK villa with a private pool after leaving this office in your brand new German car wearing the top brands of the world."

All the employees got charged up with the thrilling voice and encouraging words of Viren.

"Now jump in those manuscripts and stop only when you find the gold otherwise read till your last breath. Love you motherfuckers."

Rishabh and Angel heard everything standing near the door and once he was done with his speech they entered Viren's office.

"Oh, the man himself. Why did you bother? I would have come myself to give you a blow job. I love your money shots brother."

"Are you high?" Angel asked smilingly, bewildered with his language.

"Who is she?" Viren asked.

"My girlfriend, Angel," Rishabh said.

"What the fuck are you talking about? That's a viagratic news. It will push our sales to an orgasmic level."

Angel burst out in laughter. Rishabh had already been through that emotion many times so he was serene with a smile.

"So when did you lose your touch with normal mode of communication?" Angel asked Viren.

"When ostentatious IIM with its Godly erections started banging me without wearing a watch? But wait a minute, you are so beautiful and you behave perfectly normal in our first meeting. Where did you find her Rishabh? You both are a perfect match. What would you like to have other than my loquacity?"

"Your help," both said in unison immediately, before he gets started again.

Viren rolled his eyes and offered them the seat.

Rishabh went on explaining everything right from their meeting with Krishna.

"You guys are fucking crazy," Viren remarked after listening everything. "You are a super couple. Oh wait a minute, a book can be written on your story. Imagine the love making scene between the two people spreading so much of love, there will be a tsunami of love and love juices. It will be an instant hit."

Angel got up and started frisking Viren.

"Apart from my wife's touch, I am haptophobic, what the hell are you doing young lady?"

"I am looking for your batteries."

"Alright sit down. I got you," he said making Angel sit. "Jaggu will work for a magazine in a photography section. I will get him hooked."

They both jumped and hugged him.

11

"Excuse me," Rishabh stopped Jaggu on his way to the building in the morning. Jaggu scanned him thoroughly but did not recognize him.

"Can you please click one picture of me with this lady?" Rishabh asked with an old wrinkled lady standing beside him. He handed over his DSLR camera to Jaggu.

Jaggu held it for some time staring at it and wondering how much technology has advanced in last one and a half decade.

"Sir, Will you please click the picture?" Rishabh asked again. Jaggu clicked one picture on the camera and handed it over back to Rishabh. Lady and Jaggu started walking away.

"Excuse me," Rishabh stopped him again as he was entering the building. "Are you a photographer?"

Jaggu got baffled by the question. He treaded heavily towards Rishabh and trampled a few flowers on the way. He stood tall over Rishabh and asked him, "Who are you?"

"I am Rishabh, the editor of Laile Maro Magazine," he said with a shaking voice.

"Why did you ask me that question?"

"See it yourself," Rishabh showed him the high resolution picture. All the settings were already set. In a day light area even a 5 year old kid would have clicked a good picture with that camera.

Jaggu gave a tiniest smile for a nanosecond and then said with extreme humility, "Your camera is very good. It can make anyone a photographer". Rishabh understood that Jaggu's passion is the gate pass for humbleness to enter inside him. So he tried to open the gates fully by fingering his sensitive emotions for his passion.

"It's not just about the camera. It's the emotional touch which only a person who has been through various emotions can give to. This world is beautiful and full of emotions but everybody is so busy with their lives that they are never able to witness the miracles of the Universe. Only a photographer like you, who has got an eye for the details, can first create a picture in his mind and then capture it in a camera. Only a person who is in touch with the deepest emotions becomes the best photographer. Your eyes tell a story brother and these are the natural lenses provided by God, they never lie. Everybody has a purpose in life. Those who find it live a life worth living. I don't know what you are currently doing in your life but if you are not practicing photography, you are certainly not living your purpose. I am looking for someone who is passionate about photography. If you want to work with me, just call me," he said handing over the card and walked away hiding his palpitating heart. Jaggu stood there holding the card reminiscing over some worn-out memories placed in a rusted compartment of his brain.

"Bhiaya, bhaiya," Sharfun came running towards Jaggu. "How are you now bhaiya?"

"I am good," Jaggu smiled. "Thanks for helping me that day."

"No need to say that bhaiya. Someone helped me one day so I am just returning the favor. By the way why did you run away that day? Mom felt very bad. Please come again this evening. We will have dinner together and please don't say no. Promise me you will come."

Jaggu had to promise to that cute persuader. He looked towards the sky in amazement over the serendipity and went smiling inside the building.

12

A flower vase missed Rishabh and hit the elevator behind him.

"I am going to kill you, you lecher," Angel shouted picking up another vase.

"I will pay for that," Rishabh said to the manager of the café standing beside him who was also trying to save himself from the fury of Angel. All eyes were on them.

"You said it will be a no show, no blow thing. How can you fucking give a verbal orgasm to her?" Now all the ears went up too. "And you dare to tell me now, after two fucking days."

"It's easy. I will give you one too." Rishabh's reply invited another vase which came flying towards him. Instant reflex of Rishabh saved manager from the blow.

"Alright, alright. I will not give you." This time it came faster than the previous one and the manager would have almost kissed the vase had Rishabh not saved him again.

"What do you want Angel? Stop behaving like a kid."

"I want plenty of those verbal ones but I am going to kill you before that."

"Has she gone mad today?" Amit, the manager asked.

"Little bit horny I guess," Rishabh answered.

An old couple stood shocked inside the elevator watching the scene outside it as they reached that terrace café.

Rishabh quickly jumped inside it and pressed ground button but before it could close, Angel was inside it. After getting few punches from her, Rishabh got her hands in control and made her look into his eyes. The violent Angel was now in control and without any delay Rishabh landed his lips on hers. The couple was still in shock.

Meanwhile Jaggu reached Rehman Chacha's home. The aroma of chicken Biryani, cricket commentary on an old style CRT TV set, continuous chatter of girls, he was back home after almost twelve years. The toddler came crawling near his legs. He picked him up and started playing with him. The smile meter was all time high. It was a fun-filled family evening where Jaggu not only savored chicken Biryani, but the care of a mother for his son's appetite, the sweet chatter of sisters over anything of the world, toddler's soothing activities, the face of a content father watching his family happy and healthy. Jaggu was away from those emotions for long, Rishabh and Angel were just trying to get him in touch with those emotions.

Next day Jaggu could see cameras everywhere, with students, with foreigners, people taking selfies, inside electronic stores, everywhere. We live in a world of abundance. There is abundant information on everything surrounding us all the time but we could only see and analyze what we want at that particular time. If we plan to buy a car we would only see cars everywhere. God must be a great programmer.

"I am sorry my friend. Hey you," Rishabh said to Jaggu

after colliding with him while intentionally walking backwards to take a picture. "How are you brother?"

"I am good"

"Are you stalking me, but I gave you my card. Did you lose it?"

Before Jaggu could say something Rishabh continued, "Oh I am just kidding. What is your name by the way?"

"Jaggu"

"That's a catchy name. What do you do?"

A cargo van stopped near them with a flat wheel. The driver came out hurriedly and took out the jack.

Rishabh handing over the camera to Jaggu took the wrench from tool kit and started loosening the nuts.

"Thank you friend," the driver said.

Rishabh gave a smile and continued with his work. In less than five minutes the wheel was changed.

"Thank you so much brother. I was terribly late for delivering the order. You saved me a lot of time."

"My pleasure"

"How do you manage to make everyone smile every time?" Jaggu asked after the van was gone.

"Smiles are always appreciated, a shrewd businessman told me once. So I am just following his advice of investing a lot in them and making my future secured," Rishabh replied and there was one more investment in Jaggu's smile.

"Where did you learn photography?" Jaggu asked.

"Oh, I do not know the P of photography but my friends in Bollywood who work behind the camera tell me a few things about it."

"Like?"

"It's an art of giving a life to a picture. Learning

111

technicalities of a camera comprise only one percent, rest ninety nine percent is your emotional connect."

"Emotional connect?"

"Like if you are into food photography, you have to feel the natural color of vegetables and fruits, the rich taste of spices, the surface of various utensils in which the food is prepared, etc".

Jaggu was hearing Rishabh very patiently.

"Or say if you are into a glamour photography, you have to feel about the body and its beauty which does not mean you have to click nude pictures. Then it will be a pornography not photography."

They shared a good laugh.

"You have to open yourself to every emotion of a particular field of photography, be it journalism, wedding, landscape, wildlife, pet or crime," Rishabh pressurized on the last word. Jaggu turned away his gaze.

"I need to go now. I am getting late for some work," Jaggu said and walked away. Rishabh watched him quietly, discerning on how powerful today's hammer was to shake off the dust.

While Rishabh and Rehmaan Chacha's family kept Jaggu busy, Angel with the help of Krishna gathered all the kids to teach them with her own methods in a garden.

"Hey Krishna, you said you saw some treasure here. Where is it?" one of the boys asked Krishna.

Suddenly water bubbles with shades of rainbow surrounded all the kids. The amazed kids first gazed and then chased the bubbles to blow them up. Angel along with Sandy and his two buddies came from behind and gave a bottle filled with some liquid to each of them along with a black light.

"All right, put the bottles down and pay attention here," she said. All of them followed her commanding voice, paying attention to her beauty, her hands gesturing for standing still and her enchanting eyes looking at each of them.

"Krishna was right, you are going to find some treasure today," her pace of speech was slower than the usual.

"But do you know who gets the treasure in this world?" she asked and continued after a pause, "Only the kings and the queens. And with that treasure, they are not required to do any kind of work, they just play whole day. They can roam the world. They can eat whatever they want. They can wear beautiful clothes. Queens can do make up even when they do not have to go anywhere. Rather than asking for money, they give money to the needy and help them. They have nice and clean homes where they sleep on a big bed. They have their own vehicle, not one but many to travel from one place to another. But to have all these things in your life, you should have the treasure and to get the treasure you will have to become a king or a queen first. So who wants to be the King or the Queen?"

They all started shouting me, me, me. Raising hands was out of their syllabus.

"For that, first you will have to eliminate the darkness with light. Pick up the bottles now."

They picked up looking at each other and laughing, lifting their shoulders up.

"Now turn on the black light and focus it on the bottle" and they all were wowed at the sudden light up of the garden with those phosphors inside the bottles. The crowd nearby gathered there to witness the magic of Angel. Teaching is an

113

art and she truly was a great teacher of life lessons.

Angel knew, that the very first lesson she will have to teach them, was to live with dignity and to have a self-respect. To have a living too, these kids had to shun their dignity first. Most of the people did not even treat them as humans. Many parents moved their kids away from these vagrant kids.

They were small directionless children but they had an equal right to live a dignified life. It is an utter shame that humans have created a scenario where some kids are forced to learn begging. But Angel knew how to give their self-respect back.

"Alright, now put the bottles aside and sit down."

They readily followed their newly found teacher.

"Now to become the king or the Queen we will have to learn about their qualities first. The very important quality which they have is they never ask for anything, they always give. They are generous."

"But if we will not ask, that mother fucker Jaggu Bhaiya will make our keema (Indian non-veg food dish)," one of the kids said. Rest of them started laughing.

"Hey Munna," Krishna said. "Angel didi is here for us. Don't talk to her like that."

"It's okay Krishna," Angel said and walked towards Munna. "Jaggu can never touch anyone of you now onwards" she said looking straight into Munna's eyes, her each and every word crystal clear and razor sharp. "And kings do not say bad words. This is your first and last warning." That zipped Munna. "Sandy, please distribute the lenses."

She gave everyone a button spy camera and told them to

wear it every day.

"Till the time you wear this and promise me not to tell anyone about our meeting, I promise, no one will be able to touch you," she said.

"And remember," She continued, "from tomorrow onwards you are not going to ask for money. Rather you will present your talent to people, showcase your skills in front of them. No more crying and showing disgruntled faces to them. Rather, you will smile and give them the reason to smile," she stressed on giving. "So it's you who will be giving to them not the other way round. And that's how you will become the King or the Queen."

She then started identifying every individual kid's specific talent. Attempt was made to find the tentative field of interest of every kid by giving them free atmosphere, playing various analytical games, asking questions and interacting with them.

While kids were busy playing, Sandy asked Angel, "How can we be sure about their specific talent in such a short duration? If we go wrong, we will have Sachin Tendulkars struggling in tennis for their whole lives.

"Don't worry I won't let that happen. It's a hit and trial method. Nothing will be finalized today. The field which excites a particular kid the most, which enthralls it, motivates it to perform most number of times will be zeroed in for him or her and then our talent mentors from NGOs will guide them further once we release them from that prison."

And in few days, she found out a talent factory from that crime factory of Baba. There were singers, dancers, mimicry artists, gymnasts, comedians, beauty pageant aspirants, sportspersons, painters and musicians. She gave every kid a hundred rupee note every day. They were smart enough to dodge the people managing them and Jaggu was already in a different world. He did not care about business anymore.

While the talent hunt was still on and almost all the kids had found out their hidden talent, Munna was yet to discover his own, but despite of that he enjoyed the whole process of watching others discover their talent.

"So you are going to be a singer, dumbfuck?" Munna asked Krishna.

"Yes," Krishna replied clearing his throat. Munna gave him a bottle of water.

"You know I knew it the day when I was waiting outside the toilet for the first time when you were inside. A person who can sing so well with his asshole can obviously sing a lot better with his mouth."

"Shut up and get lost form here," Krishna shouted at him. Munna went laughing uncontrollably to Sandy.

"Sandy bhaiya," Munna called in Sandy's attention who was busy preparing database in a notebook.

"Yes Munna"

"Krishna is an amazing singer and Kaali creates a soothing music from utensils. Can we fuse their talents together?"

Sandy was impressed with the idea and told it to Angel. After that Angel started monitoring Munna's activities closely.

He used to tease everyone a lot but parallel to that he used to motivate them too, to explore something new, praise them for their efforts not their ability. Angel was a tough teacher. She made them practice without any leniency. Now practice is not easy. It requires passion, motivation, persistence and the emotional fuel we all call love. When talent is intertwined with a goal, that triggers fire and a tsunami of unconscious motivational energy is released. Munna played an instrumental role in doing so. He also helped Sandy in shifting materials and providing required resources to all other kids. Angel identified his talent and wrote 'Talent Management' against his name.

Jaggu started smiling a lot now which kids found miraculous. He did not say anything to anyone. In fact he bought chocolates and gifts for them on various occasions. He quit going to building every day, to practice photography. Every day, a feast was prepared in the mess. Kids were getting healthier now. Inadvertently, Rishabh and Angel had triggered the Baba bomb while harvesting happiness.

13

Jaggu entered in the meeting room where Baba was already sitting with three others. He was half the size of Jaggu, lean frame, but his attitude was much heavier. He was wearing a black Pathani kurta with a heavy metal bracelet on his wrist. His oil dipped hair were perfectly combed and he had a dense moustache. He preferred dark places for his dark businesses. It was a dim-lit room with an old table and few rusty chairs. A decade old fan crying its problems.

"Hey Jaggu, my little brother," Baba got up from the chair and went on to hug him. "How are you?" he asked.

"I am good Baba," Jaggu gave a nervous reply.

"It's good that you are good but it's not good that the kids are good," Baba said, his voice more stern now.

"I did not get you Baba," Jaggu stammered a little.

"Hmm. You know when I was small, I used to catch running chicken and butcher them. I haven't changed, the only difference is that now I catch lies" he said looking into Jaggu's eyes, speaking slowly. "Please do not lie to me and tell me why are you doing this?"

Jaggu gathered the courage to speak. "I want them to live a good life," he said. "They need a family. Being accepted in the society.."

"Bunch of fools form a society," Baba shouted in his loudest pitch in that meeting room. "You know this so-called society comprises of cowards. Even a small cat crossing their path scares them. You want these kids to be like them. Any half naked guy wearing saffron clothes can scare them to death, by just confronting them with small problems and then giving some idiotic solutions. They are so stupid that even after reading and learning so much they work like donkeys. My boys can make them shit in their pants. They are fools. You want these kids to be a part of this fool factory."

"At least it's better than your crime factory."

"What crime? It's a business."

"Business of selling emotions through small kids who should be going to school every morning rather than a traffic signal, who should be carrying a book rather than a bowl."

"Who doesn't sell emotions?" he said coming close to Jaggu. "Every businessman does it. Have you ever seen any car company promoting specifications of it? They always say that it's a family car with a dog in the picture," he said with a taunting tone and then gave some more examples. "The engine oil keeps this nation running and united. The mobile network service providers just want you to talk with your loved ones for whole day. How can a fucking chocolate drink increase your height or a paste of fragrant chemicals make you fair? The camera company never talks about the image quality, it says this camera captures the precious moments with your loved ones. But that's how you sell to this bunch of fools, they only understand emotions. And what school you are talking about? These books and school makes them eligible to get government license of robbing people in daylight. These fucking licensed people harass everyone out there which results in a hatred. Communal riots are a result of hatred. How can you forget the burning of your own family by other families of your so called society? There is no nobility in being accepted by the society. Fucking morons want to be a part of the society. For us, it's all about being in power. You know what power is? These three muscular men can crush me to death but they cannot do it." He then turned towards them, "Hey hit me, beat me scumbag, come on, crush me to death motherfucker" and then started laughing looking at them standing still. "See, that's called power."

"Those who burnt my family did not belong to any family. They were your creation who could do anything for money," Jaggu said slowly with tears in his eyes. "You are creating monsters who have no control over their lives. You did not give me shelter that day; you covered my devastated life with a black sheet so that it can never see the light again. I am not going to let that happen to these kids."

"I think you missed my power speech," Baba sighed and then turned to the muscular men. "Purge him," he ordered and started walking away.

Jaggu lay on floor, soaked in blood. Rishabh after hearing the conversation through a transmitter in Jaggu's jacket tracked its location on GPS. Through his contacts in media, he hospitalized Jaggu without any hassle of police investigation. Jaggu remained unconscious whole night post operation. The first thing he said in the morning after gaining consciousness was:

"Please save the kids. Baba knows that they are learning something new which can make them independent and he doesn't like it at all so tonight he will amputate them, blind them or pour acid on them. He will do whatever he can to snatch away their freedom."

Along with doctor and a nurse who were standing beside the bed, Rishabh, Angel and Inspector Iqbal Sheikh got traumatized after learning the abominable acts of Baba.

Doctor stopped Jaggu from speaking more because of the stitches on his face and told everyone to leave the room.

"How do you know him?" Iqbal asked Rishabh. He told him everything right from when he and Angel met Krishna.

"What are you going to do now?" Angel asked Iqbal.

"Listen to me very carefully. This Baba is very smart. I have big file on his name but because of big political contacts and his indirect involvement in all the crimes we are never able to catch him. Even after having Jaggu's statement, I cannot arrest him and if I arrest him they will transfer me elsewhere. Now if you want to save the kids do exactly as I say. We do not have much time left." He said and then unveiled his plan.

****

Before kids could go back to Baba from traffic signal, their beloved Angel didi and Rishabh hijacked them and provided them the banners. Within minutes the Panjrapole crossroad was blocked. At the center were kids with banners saying, "Your alms takes our arms," "Your mental blindness takes our eyes," "Your donation is acid on us," "Save us please". Traffic police could not do anything because kids were protected by college students who were the volunteers of the opposition political party. Cameras of media were doing their job. TV channels started flashing the breaking news.

A man in a white kurta and pajama sighed after watching the news.

"Give me the phone," he said to his PA in frustration.

"I am sorry Sir," Baba apologized on the phone. "I don't know how all this happened."

"Shut up motherfucker and listen to me. Get underground and come out only after elections." He disconnected the call. "Elections are just around the corner. Tell Shakti to focus more on betting business. This begging business is not going to generate any funds," he said to his PA.

An NGO took the responsibility of the kids and their education. Rishabh arranged photography classes for Jaggu in the hospital. Baba went underground resulting in the release of more kids from begging business. Inspector Iqbal went on a rampage to destroy Baba.

14

Porsche, like Google, knew already where to stop even before Rishabh applied brakes in Gandhinagar.

"I have dropped you here many a times now. Someone from the neighborhood must have tried to enquire about me."

"Yes they know you as a friend from NGO."

"Friend?" Rishabh made a sour face. "Why not boyfriend?"

"Because that news will become the breaking news, which upon reaching to my parents, will get us married within two hours."

"Is it the family genes or they are so fed up of you?"

"None. In fact they love me and trust my choice a lot and want me to settle down quickly. They know that finding a perfect match for me is a daunting task and if they will come to know that I am dating someone, without a second thought they will make you their son-in-law."

"I don't mind their two hour marriage plan by the way."

"God has increased the lease period of this planet after 2012. So we have lot of time sweetheart. And it's my marriage, not the Bolt's hundred meter track. So hold your horses and calm down."

"Tell me something more about your parents"

"Oh, I love them," she said and got engaged in her thoughts. "I love their fights."

"Fights?" Rishabh asked surprisingly.

"Oh yes, how can I forget that? Here comes the genetic part. They have loved each other so much for their whole lives that now they are experimenting it by fighting with each other randomly and then falling for each other again. And when I say fighting, I literally mean it. They even throw things at each other. Actually you should come with me. You can see it yourself. And don't get surprised if you find a broken TV or a furniture inside our home."

"Now I just can't wait to meet them but will they perform their intense love fights in front of me also?"

"Are you mad? I will keep you in hiding. They won't even know that you are at home."

"Are you crazy?"

Angel laughed like Ravana.

"I am sorry, silly question. Are you sure, I wanted to ask actually"

"Listen, here's the plan. I will bring Mom and Dad outside home and walk them away after cooking some story. By that time you get inside and reach my room upstairs. There is only one room there so no confusion. Now go and hide in the bushes."

Rishabh parked his car far away from her home and waited in the dark for her signal to get in.

"Mom, Dad, I found him," she screamed in the house.

Her parents came running out of a kitchen. Her father, a tall, clean shaven, well-built guy in his late forties wearing a white collared tee over a black track pant had bathed in a wheat floor while her mother wearing a turquoise satin gown, well maintained, little older version of Angel got her head ornate with vegetable peels.

"Take this," they said handing out a Mangalsutra (wedding necklace) and a box of sindoor (vermillion).

"Where is he?" her father asked searching around Angel.

"In the bushes," Angel answered smiling with excitement.

"Bushes?" her mom asked. "Why so shy? Call him in, I will call panditji till then."

"Calm down mom. He is a bunny."

Father laughed. "Another fan of Ranbir Kapoor (Bollywood actor) like me. So what is his real name?"

Angel sighed. "He is a rabbit Dad. I saw a rabbit in the bushes."

"Oh," they both held ears saying "Sorry"

"But how do you know it's a male?" father asked.

"He was small. Female rabbits are bigger in size and dominant. Now come on, let's find him," she said and all three went outside the house for searching an illusionary rabbit.

"So, it's not only humans who are facing this dominance issue," her father said taunting her mother while they walked outside their home.

"One more excuse to shove the fact down in the guts that he has got a way too smart wife in whose presence he feels dominated and feeble", said mother with a phony anger.

"You should go a little deeper in the bushes. The bunny

might come out smelling your vegetation."

While they were playing with each other's hormonal levels, Angel signaled Rishabh to move inside.

Rishabh graciously walked inside the home without touching anything.

"One more trite comment. People can see who is vegetating," Angel's mother said.

"That's the problem with you, you never understand me. I was talking about the vegetables on your head."

"Swear on Angel's rabbit that you were talking about vegetables."

"Hey, hey, hey," Angel interrupted. "Keep my rabbit out of it. He is way too cute to take the burden of your swear and by the way I think he reached home safely. Let's go."

They started walking back inside home.

"You know when people tend to lose debate, they come down to swears," Angel's father sparked her mother again.

"That's it. Tonight I will show you what dominance is."

"Really," he said excitedly. "Actually night is the only time I like your dominance. Do you remember our honeymoon in Shimla?"

"Of course I remember. How can I forget the place where I conceived my sweet little Angel?"

"Bathtub to be precise."

"Boundaries, my dear parents, boundaries," Angel tried to control her parents but in vain.

"No darling, I think it was the tent while camping."

Angel surrendered and quickly went towards her room while they walked slowly behind her, discussing the location.

Her room was a research and development center of craziness or a laboratory of creativity. The floor was designed as if you were walking in a fresh water with smooth pebbles inside it. A teddy performing gravity defying Malkhama (pole gymnastics) with a thumbs up, a sparkling smile and a blinked eye. A set of stringed small metal balls which generated different waveforms. A big handmade clock with a picture of Angel with various expressions on every number. One wall was dedicated to personalities like Mark Twain, Gautam Buddha and Mahatma Gandhi for sharing their wisdom. Rishabh was still exploring her room when she came running inside.

"Rishabh come here," she called him near the door. "Now just listen to them for a while," she kept the door slightly open.

"For once I can believe about the first class train compartment but how can you conceive in a trolley car?" her Dad argued.

"You always do this, you never listen to me. That night of our honeymoon also you did not get me an ice cream."

"Who in their right mind would ask for an ice cream at 2 am in a freezing three degree Celsius?"

"All men are like that. Moon and stars are for sale before marriage and after marriage even a small ice cream becomes a herculean task."

Rishabh started rolling on floor laughing in mute.

"Really?" Angle said smiling at Rishabh. "But they are just warming up."

"Your parents are damn cute. I love them" he said sitting on the floor after controlling his laughter with his arms wrapped around his knees. "Now please make them sleep so that I can leave or else they will find me out with my laughter. I can't control it much."

"You are not going anywhere tonight."

"What do you mean?"

She gave a mysterious smile and then shouted outside the door, "Mom, Dad, enough for today. Go to sleep now."

"Alright sweetheart," her Dad replied.

"Good night darling," her mother said and it was a total silence.

She shut the door and said, "You are hijacked"

"Pleasure is all mine," Rishabh said.

She walked slowly towards him as if she was breakable, unlocked his arms wrapped around knees and sat in his accommodating lap, her legs wrapped around his waist and her arms around his neck.

She roughly moved her hand through his hair and said, "Thanks for coming into my life Rishabh" and she felt his forehead on her lips. "You make me feel beautiful in a way that I lose the focus of the world around me". She hugged him and whispered in his ear, "I love you."

He took a deep breath and felt more of her. "I love you too," he said and held her tight.

Their eyes were now relentlessly locked into each other showing so many emotions; love, concern, passion, adoration, erotic desire. He looked at her as if she was the only woman on earth, as if there was nothing in their private universe.

"You know," she said. "In these past few days, your heroism has made me release so much of oxytocin, I think the feast is ready."

Some 200 gigahertz processor produced an instant smile on Rishabh's face.

His hand tangled in her hair, gently tugging her face to

his. A feeling of tremor ran through both of them. The magnetic force today was so fierce that it resulted in a passionate kiss with exploring tongues.

He got up with she wrapped around him, still kissing. She switched off the lights without unlocking the lips while Rishabh walked her towards the bed. That creative ground of Angel converted into a planetarium, a perfect place to make love.

He made her lay on the bed comfortably. She looked magnificent, her long dark hair spread out across the white pillow, her eyes full and deep, locked on his. He started peeling off her beautifully embraced white top over her glistening curves. A round of planting passionate kisses started from down her neck to her shoulders to her navel. She felt his hair caressing her body while he explored her navel. She heard her own slow moans fly unbidden from her throat. Down her waist she tightened like a knot pulled just too tight.

She started unbuttoning his black shirt which in a way was pleading for mercy to her torture of going insane. Her fingers started exploring the so longed love making body of Rishabh. Beneath her touch she found a sculpted masculine figure in action.

Rishabh loved her moaning and panting along with planting passionate kisses which spurred him on and despite of feeling too much of her it encouraged him to explore more and more of her. In no time, they found themselves in their most natural form without any clothes on.

She opened her gates to the origin of mankind, for him to enter, and smiled. He felt her smile travel all the way to his heart. Entering the gates was uncomfortable at first but once he was in, it was blissfulness all the way. For her it was painful but the sensation of having him inside her, the emotions she saw on his face, in his eyes, distracted her from the twinges inside.

Watching her in pain, he said, "I am sorry, it was the worst one I promise". She smiled and said, "Welcome home Rishabh."

He bent down to reach the mouth which said the magical words.

They kept loving each other, every movement, every yearning reflecting in their eyes. Her tightened grip indicated her pleasure. She already had so much of him that any explosive oozing would be a bonus in addition to what she felt, when they conjoined.

In the climax, when they reached the zenith of their intense love making, it was a free fall after that, during which they held each other as if not letting each other go anywhere from that sacred space created by them.

15

Shyna was a virago. In her first meeting with Viren, she proposed him and when he asked for a day to think over, she grabbed him by his balls. He instantly fell in love and pain at the same time. They complemented each other's personality so well that wherever they went they became the agents of chaos. Marriages are made in heaven but this one must have been made when heaven managers were drunk and they partied so hard that the hell residents would have sent a bulk of pleas requesting one more chance of spending a sober life on earth just to attend this one kickass party of heaven.

When Rishabh and Angel reached the sprawling mansion of Viren and Shyna, Angel was spell bound by its substantial size. A Land Rover was parked near the gate followed by a lush garden. On the other side of the walkway was a plush private pool defined with some artistic beauty, but the house inside was a total mess. There was furniture everywhere. Shyna was an interior designer and she was decorating their new house. Even after six years of marriage she carried an envious figure. May be it was her seductive techniques that charged up Viren every morning, after spending pleasurable nights with her, to run for the seven figure income he made every month.

"Mahogany you fool, M for motherfucker, M for mahogany," she shouted on someone on the call.

A chequered red shirt over white shorts, the two glistening sexy legs carrying plethora of curves and attitude, the straight picturesque waterfall like hair from behind with a perfect 180 degree haircut, she was an Indian version of Victoria Beckham.

"And how much time does it take to make a fucking table. Send it by tomorrow or else I am going to release few of those drones behind your ass," she disconnected the call.

"Spare the poor humans sweetheart," Rishabh said as they entered the house.

"Hey, the Literary Rock star Rishabh. How are you darling?" she said as she hugged him, "I am sorry about the call."

"It's okay. The hotness has to vent out somewhere."

"Look who is here," she said looking at Angel. "The guest of the evening. My God, she is so pretty, I was just dying to meet you after hearing so much about you," she said and hugged her.

"I don't know what have you heard of me but whatever I saw of you right now, I am sure you are being generous with me. You are a mine of artilleries, few others like you together can create a havoc on those tiny countries."

"Where did you find her Rishabh?" she asked Rishabh without keeping her gaze off Angel.

"Right where the staircase from the heaven ends."

"Oh my dear favorite writer, you just gave me a clit boner."

All three shared a laugh.

"Where is Viren?" Angel asked.

"He has become like low grade mobile network these days, disappearing all the time. He is behaving like a total dick, gets up anytime and starts working. Today also I told him to be on time but see, no Viren till now. I am not going to leave him today."

"Whatever you do, don't kick his balls," Rishabh quipped.

"He wears a guard after that incident," she said. "I mean except the bedroom of course," she finished.

Angel was amused by Shyna. She was totally enjoying her newly found entertainment.

"Somebody missed me," Viren came with shopping bags, smiling all the way.

"Yes, the iron rod placed outside missed your asshole actually. I told you to be on time, you fucktard. Where were you?"

"The main engine of Mangalyaan had some issues so they called me for some expert advice. Where do you think I was? I was at my office giving blow jobs to my clients."

"This is my house and you will have to stay here by my rules. You are not going to work on Sundays," Shyna commanded. Viren's phone started ringing. "And you are not going to pick that fucking call."

"I will have to take that," Viren said looking somberly at his cellphone.

"Decide where do you want to slide your finger? On that motherfucking monster in your hand or in my pussy."

Rishabh and Angel tried to find a chance to pacify them

but the ferocity of their altercation was too high to act as a mediator.

"If you want your pussy to be fingered in the luxurious bedroom of this lavish mansion rather than a petty bedroom of a 2BHK apartment with 400 other apartments around you, please let me take this fucking call on a fucking Sunday in front of my friends invited for a dinner watching this fucked up situation," he said in a single breath. All three watched him with their jaw on ground.

Catching up his breath he said again, "Baby, some stupid man said, diamonds are woman's best friends and these bags contain a lot of that stupidity. Now please, can I pick this call?"

"Give me the bags sweetheart, you must be tired," Shyna said calmly.

He gave the bags and picked up the call while walking towards the garden.

Angel accompanied Shyna with the bags while Rishabh waited to catch up with Viren.

"Bro, you can expect the big news," Viren said to Rishabh after disconnecting the call. "Rajkumar Hirani was heard talking about you."

Meanwhile Shyna screamed so loud that they had to run inside leaving the news aside.

"This necklace is a beauty sweetheart. I love you," Shyna said to Viren as they reached inside.

"It has to be. I have given almost a kilo of a blow for that," Viren replied.

"Oh darling, I am really sorry. You work so hard for us and I lash at you."

"It's okay baby. Come here, I need an emergency kiss."

She jumped over him and grabbed his lips. They kissed like crazy.

"You want some quicky baby," Shyna asked hanging onto him. Viren looked at Rishabh and Angel as if asking for permission.

"Of course," Rishabh said. "Make yourself home. We are absolutely fine." Angel gave a thumbs up.

They kept kissing and moving sporadically towards the bedroom. Rishabh and Angel savored their explosive chemistry.

After that quick quicky, they gathered at the dinner table placed in the garden outside their home. Shyna looked fabulous in her black designer outfit and the glittering necklace that Viren bought for her. Viren was always in suits. Rishabh's uniform of black shirt and blue denims was classy and Angel looked adorable in pink kurti and white churidaar. The table with scrumptious food and champagne was set with four amazing characters ready to savor it with some spicy conversation.

Shyna raised the toast, "to the good times". "To the good times," everybody said.

"I really feel blessed to have you both in my life. You two make such a lovely couple," Angel said.

"Oh the feeling is mutual dear," Shyna said. "You know when I look at you and Rishabh I get this blissful feeling which is so pure like an orgasm. It's like.."

"And the award for the obscene conversation over the dinner table goes to Shyna," Viren announced and started ringing the glass with a spoon. Everybody laughed.

"But seriously I too admire your relationship a lot," Rishabh said. "The way you have supported Viren from his

135

struggle to his success is commendable."

"Please don't make me cry sweetheart, I will have to wash away my expensive Paris make up."

"Now I can't wait to listen to your story," Angel said.

"Oh there is no story," Viren said. "She grabbed my balls and all I remember after that is holding a ball pen in a court room. I never knew that one signature would change my life. When I left my high paying job to pursue a career in my interest of reading books, I was swarmed with those anaconda like challenges. I used to look at life from a different angle. God sent her into my life and she held me from the most delicate part of my body and took me out of those challenges by shifting my angle of depression to the angle of elevation. She is the source of my motivation and my energy. She is the reason of my existence," Viren said looking into Shyna's eyes. She was already in tears making her eyes shine along with the diamonds. They hugged and kissed each other.

Rishabh and Angel kept looking at them with a smiling face in their hands, supported by an elbow on the table.

"That one signature truly changed your life Viren," Rishabh said.

"Exactly and you two also should not delay the process. Have you spilled the beans to your parents yet?" Viren asked.

"Nah," they both said in unison.

"So what are you guys waiting for? I know Rishabh's parents, they amazing people and Rishabh has told me about your parents too. It's easy. Everything is going to be smooth. What's the problem?"

"Smooth is the problem?" Angel's crazy cells became active.

"Tighten your seat belt guys. She is going to take you off," Rishabh warned.

"What do you mean Angel?" Shyna asked with a grave concern.

"I don't like smooth. It's boring. I am going to marry only once. What story will I tell to my offspring? That your father and I fell in love, proposed each other, our parents agreed and we got happily married. No way," she rejected the smooth plan.

"You can tell them anything," Viren said. "Those tit suckers believe everything. You can tell them the world population was 79 billion before the Armageddon happened but how you and Rishabh heroically survived everything and brought them into this world."

"And then make them laughing stock amongst their friends," Shyna replied giggling and enjoying her drink.

"We can run a plea on social media for maintaining this secret with the upcoming generation," Viren said. "How do you think they pulled off the biggest epics ever written on this planet? Who knows whether anyone really landed on moon or not? Who knows whether Al-Qaeda is for real or it is just a creation for selfish motives?"

"That's why sometimes I feel like some kid is fucking me on a bed," Shyna said in awe of Viren's justification.

"That kid has got Thor's hammer baby," Viren replied.

"I have a rather simple plan Viren," Angel beamed.

"Please shoot sweetie and save us from his verbal assault," Shyna said.

"Step one, we impress each other's parents," Angel said.

"Oh that's a cakewalk," Shyna said. "Rishabh's parents like everyone. Once they were gung-ho about how gracefully the thief robbed them. They were all praise for him."

"And I am sure Rishabh too can easily impress your parents. What's step two," Viren said.

"Step two, they get so much impressed that they themselves talk about our marriage."

"Perfect, short and sweet story of an arranged marriage for your kids. Let's have a toast," Viren said.

"Step three," Angel interrupted Viren. "We fight like crazy in front of our parents and make them fight too. We fight like we never want to meet again. In fact, we do not want to see each other's face too."

Rishabh knew where this was going while Viren and Shyna watched Angel jaw dropped. No one spoke for some time.

"And step four?" Shyna asked finally breaking the screaming silence.

"I don't know other steps except the last one that we get happily married. We will act according to the situation plus we have Rishabh, he can take us out from any damn situation."

"You are crazy," Shyna said the clichéd.

"That would be an understatement," Viren said. "She is the mother of crazy. Her kids would be named as Crazion or Crazina. If they ever discover a planet called crazy she would be the undisputed president of it."

"Let's name this covert mission as project Crazigasm," Shyna said.

"And the award for the most lecherous lady in the home goes to Shyna," Viren announced again.

"What are you thinking Rishabh?" Angel asked watching him contemplating over something.

"Your parents must have conceived you in a roller coaster."

Laughter erupted in that garden making it shimmer in the evening.

16

Rishabh's parents took voluntary retirement from their banking jobs when Rishabh entered into a corporate world after finishing his graduation. For five years while Rishabh was away from home busy writing his success story, they pursued their interest of doing nothing and living a nomadic life away from home. They mostly travelled in a hippie style on an Enfield. His father was interested in food while mother in the culture of various villages. They were polyglot and could easily mingle with people. They believed in gift economy and kept donating from their savings on regular basis and receiving the gifts in parallel.

Once Rishabh was back home after quitting his job to pursue full time writing, they also settled down but once in a while they would go out hitchhiking or just hit the road on Enfield and today was that day.

In a black leather jacket and pepper salt hair shades, he looked nothing less than a tall and dapper George Clooney, while she resembled suave Demi Moore in that loose white shirt and rugged faded denims. As they walked out of their house with Ray Ban glasses on, the air was filled with plethora of style. If style was a subject in curriculum, they would have a doctorate in it. As he turned the ignition on, Enfield roared to life and they went on to collect some more brownie points for doing something which they liked. God has his own way of giving the brownie points to those who follow their heart and their dreams.

Rishabh's father believed life is too short to miss any feeling or feel an emotion multiple times. It could be as simple as smelling a flower, being lost for a while in its fragrance and its beauty and being thankful to Almighty for having felt the magic. Her mother loved her father's company. She used to tell him frequently that his wisdom makes her fall for him all over again.

They reached a small village near Rajkot and the first thing Rishabh's father saw was the kathiyawadi food in a roadside restaurant.

"How are you Gordhanbhai?" he greeted a guy on a reception counter counting notes.

"I am good Sir. God has been kind," he replied, smiling and greeting by joining both his hands keeping the notes aside.

"I was here last time and you fed us with finger licking food and the butter milk was out of the world."

"Thank you Sir. It would be my pleasure to serve you again. Please have a seat, I will arrange for your food."

They sat outside the restaurant with an arrangement of tables and chairs on that cloudy day, enjoying the rustic beauty of the village.

"Did you talk to him?" she asked.

"Of course I did. In fact I showed him few profiles also but he did not show any interest. I don't know what the problem is with this generation? They analyze a lot."

"I think we should give him some more time and space. He is my sagacious son."

"But how much time? I was a father already by his age."

The just begun conversation came to a halt when a muscular Yamaha R1 stopped outside that restaurant and when Angel took off her helmet all the eyes were glued to that stunner.

The brown jacket and the long neck shoes were steal of the scene but the great robbery was yet to begin. Angel was to rob them off the question of their conversation she herself was the answer to.

"Are you guys bikers too?" she asked placing her helmet on the table and watching their biking kit.

"Yes dear," Rishahbh's mother replied with a smile.

"Awesome. Gordhanbhai, one thali for me too," she shouted. "So where are you guys headed to?"

"Nowhere and everywhere, I guess," Rishabh's father said.

"What do you mean?"

"He and I search for those small little things that define life. We just follow their trails on our frequent excursions," Rishabh's mother said with humbleness in her voice.

"Doing something like that, together in this age, you guys have got me instantly hooked with you. I am Angel by the way," she said exuberantly.

"Ajay"

"Madhu"

She shook hands with them and the food arrived.

"How about yourself? Where are you headed to in life?" Ajay asked.

"I am headed towards light, to some more laughter, to a

142

place where love is the necessity of survival, where sun shines more and birds chirp more, where hatred is an alien word"

"Where stupidity is embraced and failure is respected," Rishabh said over the microphone thereby guiding Angel with her speech. "Where grass is greener and thoughts are cleaner, where life and death are equally celebrated, where monotonous is out of fashion"

"And smiles are never out of stock," Angel copied Rishabh. "Where music is worshipped with a ritual of dancing, where ignorance is given equal importance as knowledge so as to practice humbleness and shed dogmatism and skepticism, where common sense is not philosophized, where only fear would be of standing in front of God with the unused talent that he gave as a precious gift, where violence can only be seen while killing greed, anger and ego, where being in service is the highest ranked profession, where you feel blissful while having the buttermilk of Gordhanbhai and talking philosophy to the dashing couple," Angel said after Rishabh.

"They are really dashing," she said to Rishabh over microphone. "I mean you are such a lovely gorgeous looking couple," she said to his parents, "that I couldn't resist myself from meeting you. Hope I am not making you bored," she covered her blunder.

"It was a near miss, Miss beautiful," Rishabh said.

"Bored?" Rishabh's father accentuated. "You are like a visual poetry to me, like you just walked the red carpet from heaven to enlighten us, the oldies, with your golden words of wisdom. Meeting you is like excursion bonanza. You got off from that bike to take us to the paradise. Your words were like bazooka on brain that exploded the potion of blissful truth. You threw a knot carved out of string of your words and captured my heart young lady."

"Thank God he stopped," Rishabh said. "I never knew of his flirting talent. I kind of felt jealous of him right now."

"Why did you stop? You were so good?" Angel encouraged him. Rishabh's eyes opened wide.

"Ruthless," Rishabh murmured.

"It's ok dear. Too much of excitement might be dangerous for his coronary," mother said.

"You are a savior mom," Rishabh said.

They all shared a good laugh.

"By the way what do you do other than heading to utopia?" father asked.

"My parents are searching a groom for me, so before marriage I am ticking the list, you know, things to do before you die kind of a list. This solo biking was just one of them". Their ears went up listening to Angel.

"*Do you still want to give some more time and space to your son?*" father asked the mother through telepathy.

She answered with a resounding, "*Fuck, no*"

"*Since when did you started using the F word,*" he asked.

"*Either he is marrying this girl or he can remain single for his whole life. It's a final verdict of his mother.*"

"*But we are modern-age parents, we can't impose our decision onto him like that.*"

"Hello," Angel made a click sound with her fingers disrupting the connection of telepathy. "What happened? It's just a list. I am not going to die after marriage."

"What qualities you want in your husband dear?" mother asked.

"I want a writer."

Rishabh's mother tapped her palm on table exultantly.

"Calm down Madhu. Excitement can affect your coronary too," father said. "She likes writers too," he clarified to Angel.

"They have this ability to go into the details," Angel said, "to minutely observe things. They can handle any situation they are put into with a lot of maturity."

"You are giving me a boner in front of my Parents sweetheart," Rishabh said over the microphone.

"They are the ones who record our past and foresee our future," Angel recalled Viren's words.

"Alright, go on. Embarrass me," Rishabh said.

"When God was preparing them in His big bowl, He mixed a lot of intelligence from His secret ingredients. A writer in your life makes you feel special in your adversity and keeps you grounded in prosperity. His knowledge is like your private pool wherein you can jump in anytime and soothe your soul," Angel described passionately.

"I can find a writer for you," father said jubilantly.

"Really?" Angel asked with a pretentious curiosity.

"Of course, I have lot of connections in the fraternity. I will find the best one for you. Give me your contact details please."

"Great job agent Angel," Rishabh said.

They exchanged numbers and savored the Gujarati food.

17

Plugged catalytic converter is an important component of a car exhaust system. It needs to be kept clear to let the exhaust out. If it gets clogged, the engine has to work harder requiring more acceleration because exhaust is backing up in the pipe. And that can result in a power failure and stalling. Poor Angel's parents did not understand this mechanics and Rishabh took advantage of it, obviously with accomplice Angel.

"What happened?" Rishabh asked Angel's father.

"She cheated on me," he said looking at his car. Angel's mother started observing Rishabh.

"These species need extra attention, Sir. But don't worry, mine is in good mood today. You can ride on her," Rishabh said indicating towards his black convertible Porsche.

"She is a beauty," he rejoiced walking towards it leaving behind his wife.

"You can walk with me beautiful lady," Rishabh tried to be chivalrous with her imminent mother in law. She smiled in awe of his charming looks and polished behavior.

"She is so sexy. This is what I call lust at first sight," father said.

"Go easy Sir. She can take you high."

"I would love to go on a ninth cloud with her."

"Don't listen to him son. Can you please drop us to Nehrunagar?" mother asked politely.

"Of course, please have a seat."

"I will sit in front," mother said. "Such a handsome man deserves a lady on the front seat."

"That's really thoughtful of you," Rishabh said while opening the door for her.

"Strange world. Everybody likes other's lady more," father murmured while hopping on a back seat and eying around the sexy car. "Wow that's a lovely hat," he said.

"Oh no, don't touch that," Rishabh said but it was too late. As soon as Angel's father took that noticeably stylish hat, a rabbit jumped out of it. The open hood convertible Porsche made it easy for it to jump out of it in a nearby garden.

"Oh I am so sorry son, I did not know the hat was pregnant with a rabbit."

"Shut up," Angel's mother said. "Why can't you keep your hands in control?"

"My hands love to explore the unexplored areas and you too like them doing so. You remember that night when I came home drunk."

"Oh shut up you pervert. Just go and find the rabbit."

"But sweetheart I do not know how to catch a rabbit."

"Don't worry," Rishabh smiled. "I know how to find it but I need your support for that."

"Anything dear. Just tell us what can we do for you?"

"Let's walk"

Rather than entering into the garden, Rishabh lead them

to the straight path.

"The rabbit is in the garden son," mother said.

"It's useless to run after it."

"Then how are we going to catch it?" father asked.

"Rabbit is like happiness. Most of us run after our rabbits out of a habit not realizing that happiness is fleeting. It runs away just like that. Now to get it back first thing we should do is to stop chasing it."

"Then how can we get the happiness? I mean the rabbit," mother asked as they kept walking that enlightening path.

"First of all we need to know the truth, which one is a real rabbit?" Rishabh said taking a rabbit toy from a stall of roadside vendor and then put it down. "Stop being enamored by the fake rabbits. Only the real rabbit gives us the mental peace. Now dreams are like carrots and when you find your carrots, happiness comes running towards you. So to get the happiness you should run after your dreams."

"Where can we get carrots brother?" Rishabh asked a guy walking past him.

"I am afraid nowhere. In this season it's impossible to get the carrots."

"Thank you brother," Rishabh said and started walking again. Angel's parents followed him like small kids.

"Such people are known as dream stealers. Stay away from them. You will find many of them during your journey of chasing carrots. Whenever you meet them just pick up your legs and run as fast as you can. Run till they get out of sight. Do you have carrots brother?" Rishabh asked a vegetable vendor.

"No Sir I have got bottle gourd. Shall I pack it for you?"

"No thanks brother," he said as Angel's parents kept

listening to the pearls of Rishabh. "Each day will become a series of conflicts between the carrot and a bottle gourd, the right way and the easy way. You may get tempted to get that bottle gourd, to follow the least resistance path, to follow what's comfortable, what's safe, what they call as common sense. Carrots?" he asked another vendor.

"No Sir. Do you want brinjal?"

"No thank you," he said and kept walking. "Hold that temptation to settle for less because that's phase one and from there, it's only going to get tougher. Be determined what you want. Never ever settle for anything less than your dreams because easy way will always be there, ready to wash you away. Carrot?" Rishabh asked the third vendor. He nodded negatively gesturing his open palm giving "are you stupid?" kind of look.

"I think it's time to stop chasing our dreams?' mother said.

"Remember, this is a game where opponents are your fears, your doubts, your insecurities, all lined up like a firing squad ready to shoot you out of the sky. But don't lose heart, while they are not easily defeated they are far from invincible. The opponent is inside you, shouting loud to move back, tempting you to take the easy way. Shut off that loud temptation under the voice of your own heartbeat. Burn it with the fire inside you, but never let your dream die. Protecting it is your responsibility."

He stopped at a stall of another vendor and asked, "I really need carrots today anyhow. Can you please tell me where can I get them?"

"Only at Abdulbhai's, just few hundred meters from here in the main vegetable market."

"Thanks," he said. "And when you increase your efforts without losing your faith and belief in your dreams, you get a ray of hope."

Angel's parents started liking Rishabh's collocation between the carrot and the dreams, the rabbit and the happiness.

"And don't forget to have a little bit of fun," Rishabh said catching the ball and giving it back to the kids playing cricket. He then helped an old guy lift a jute bag onto his carriage, "and be humble and helpful," he said.

Angel's parents had a twinkle in their eyes when they received carrots from Abdulbhai.

"When you achieve your dreams go back to the place from where it all started," he said.

Rishabh lined up the carrots in the garden and kept a bunch of it with himself at the center. After waiting for a while, the rabbit came out of the bushes running towards him. Angel's parents were enthralled to experience the majestic interpretation of Rishabh over life through a simple example of catching a rabbit.

"This rabbit was a gift to me and now it's my duty to share this happiness with others," he said while handing over the rabbit to Angel's mother.

She was more than happy to hold it in her hands. She looked like she had achieved Nirvana. "I will give it to Angel," she said.

"Are you married?" Angel's father asked. Rishabh's excitement punched his internals.

"Nah, my parents are searching a bride for me."

"No need now," mother said.

"Sorry?" Rishabh asked in question.

"She meant to say you are the best. No need to search, the best will find you."

Rishabh dropped them at Nehrunagar but they were so ecstatic after meeting Rishabh that they forgot to ask his name and take his contact details.

18

They along with the rabbit entered the bungalow in sector 22 quietly, smiling with a sparkling light of enlightenment shining on their foreheads, rabbit's too.

"Where did you find him?" Angel jumped from a sofa in a living room to take the rabbit from the mother.

"A great soul driving Porsche gave it to us," her father said solemnly looking up in imagination.

Angel took the rabbit from her mother and started playing with it. It was super cute. "What's the address of that soul? I want to send a thank you letter. And what happened to you guys? You look pathetic when not fighting," she said walking towards the sofa cuddling with rabbit knowing that she had deliberately put them into a fight after Rishabh already told her that they forgot to take his contact details.

The light of enlightenment fade away as they saw a question mark on each other's face.

"It's your fault, I was busy with the rabbit, you should have taken his contact details," she snorted.

"If somebody farts in Burkina Faso right now that's also my fault. Blaming is the first step of giving away the control of your life," her father said furiously. "And how did you conceal this secret for twenty seven years of our marriage that your brain is in your hands, that handles a rabbit and forgets to take the contact details."

"Of all the beings, living or dead, in water, air, above or beneath the land on this planet, you are the dumbest of them all. When I hold a rabbit which tends to move, the major part of my brain is involved to handle it with care. How could I have focused on taking his contact details?"

"Oh really? How about the minor part then? Oh I am so sorry, I forgot that it resigned few years back due to overexposure to insanity."

"So finally you agree that you are insane."

"Only if insane is encoded for intelligent."

Angel was completely engrossed in that small wonder with long pink ears and constantly moving nose.

"Go, savor your intelligence on the rocks. Mix a little courtesy to stop this nonsense altercation with me and find his details for the sake of our beloved daughter."

"Whose details mom?" Angel asked.

"We found him Angel," her father said running towards her along with her mother.

"He is perfect for you Angel," her mother said as they reached towards her on sofa.

"Oh not again, please"

"His eyes were so expressive," her mother said.

"His thoughts were so noble," her father said.

"His smile was like virgin galactic taking you off to a different world," her mother said remember him in her thoughts.

"His understanding of life and its true happiness was remarkable," her father lost in thoughts too.

"He has a great heart," her mother could not stop.

"And a 420 horse power black metallic convertible Porsche with a top speed of 306 kilometer per hour reaching zero to hundred in 4.5 seconds."

Both the ladies kept looking at him for a while.

"Alright, fix a meeting with him. I want to meet him first."

The question mark reappeared on their faces with an angry emoticon.

"It's your fault, I was busy with the rabbit. You should have taken the contact details," she grunted again.

19

"Rishabh, what are you writing these days?" Ajay, Rishabh's father asked him over dinner.

"I am copying a lot of my empty mind on blank pages, Dad."

"Why, what happened?" mother asked.

"I don't know, they call it a writer's block. You get no imagination, no thoughts, no good lines, you are in a black hole."

"Oh that's a terrible place to be. How to get out of it?" mother asked.

"Travel a lot," father said. "Drink some beer, meet new people, fall in love, get married.

"Yes marriage opens new avenues," mother said. "You get refreshing thoughts on the way, you connect to another soul every moment of your life."

Rishabh enjoyed their conversation along with a meal.

"It's a blissful journey of being in touch with profound emotions and discovering each other's best traits," the writer's father said.

"Even the struggles are blissful. In fact, that is the time when you get in sync with each other and unleash the hidden powers of a true relationship."

"Alright, who is she this time?" Rishabh asked finally.

"Angel," they said in unison.

"Every girl is an angel to you. What's her name?"

"Her name is Angel," mother said.

"Her voice was so sweet," father said.

"Her eyes were so playful," mother said.

"Her thoughts were so positive," father said.

"I just can't forget her refreshing face," mother said.

"and her Yamaha R1 1000CC, 6 gear with a top speed of 285 kilometer per hour fully loaded beast."

Like R1, the gulabjamun (Indian sweet dish) travels faster from a platter to the mouth to the stomach but it stopped with a screeching brakes in Rishabh's mouth after hearing his father's words.

"Her enigmatic smile was a stress buster," mother went on unruffled. "Her mesmerizing flair with which she got off the bike."

Rishabh kept smiling thinking about her hypnotic girlfriend.

20

Like Gandhi Ashram and Jama Masjid, Riverfront has become the identity of Ahmedabad. Rishabh and Angel took their parents out for a walk nearby Sabarmati River that evening, who were inadvertent of the fact that their children are arranging their own marriage, an arranged love marriage.

"We should do this more often. It feels good," said Angel's father as they walked on riverfront enjoying the breezy evening."

"We would have felt better if you had taken his contact details," her mother snapped.

"If you want me to jump into the river, say it directly please."

"No, please don't jump into the river," Angel's mother said.

"Ah, whatever you say but you still care about me, don't you?" Angel's father asked smilingly.

"Not at all. I want you to jump into a dried lake full of crocodiles."

With expanded nostrils, he said, "No problem sweetheart. I don't know how to swim but I know how to tackle crocs. I have been living with one for a long time?"

"I have never seen such an insightfulness of life at such a tender age," Rishabh's father said as Rishabh's family approached Angel's at a distance.

"I just can't wait to do tittle-tattle with my daughter-in-law."

"We all will go on a road trip, it will be so much fun," Rishabh's father said.

'Be ready. My parents are overexcited to take you home,' Rishabh texted Angel.

'Save yourself. Mine are ready to eat you,' she replied.

Both families came face to face. Four pair of eyes fell on Rishabh and Angel, two each, sending the *target found* signal to the brain, which in return sent a signal to the vocal chords to use all the available carbohydrates.

"Angellllllllll"

"Rabbiiiiiiiit"

It was similar to Eureka moment of Archimedes. Rishabh and Angel were prepared to handle the explosive euphoria of each other's parents.

Rishabh's mother ran to hug Angel like she knew her since ages. Watching her again, Rishabh's father was delighted to the core. "Meet our son Rishabh," he said but both of them were astonished to see their son being covered by Angel's parents. They grabbed him left and right. They embraced him with closed eyes and curved lips.

"Those would be my parents," Angel said as Rishabh's parents kept watching them.

"What's your name son?" Angel's mom asked, eyes still closed, hands still grabbing his right shoulder, head still placed on right arm.

"Rishabh"

"Where are your parents?" Angel's father asked holding left of Rishabh.

"With your lovely daughter," Rishabh's mom's words opened their eyes.

They congratulated each other for an amazing production and went gaga about each other's child.

They all sat in a garden. Rishabh and Angel talked over telepathy and enjoyed watching their parents bond over a coffee.

"How did you name your daughter so perfectly? You know the way she describes some real truths of life, only an angel can do that," Rishabh's father felt gratified while saying that.

"Your son is a true master. At such a small age he knows the exact formula to achieve the dreams in life," Angel's mother said.

"Law of attraction is awesome. The secret works like a wonder. We were looking for a girl for Rishabh and who else could be better than Angel," Rishabh's mother said.

"The court must be closed now. Shall we go to the temple?" Angel's father expedited the process.

"Ok. I will get the Mangalsutra and Sindoor," Rishabh's father raised the accelerator.

"We got it already," Angel's mother put on the nitrous.

Telepathy interrupted, Rishabh and Angel got up immediately to apply some brakes to the jet speed.

"They are in a more hurry than us," Angel's mom said looking at them standing instantly.

"No way. We need to know each other first," Angel made a feeble attempt to slow down the jetliners.

"Of course," Rishabh corroborated.

"Go take a round then, we are waiting. I know a temple with 24X7 pundit available," Rishabh's mother said.

They acquiesced like small kids in front of their martinet parents.

"These parents nowadays I tell you," Angel said to Rishabh as they started walking.

They moved out of the river front park, hand in hand, trying to keep themselves afloat in a pool of imminent happiness in their lives.

****

"One thousand bucks for kissing," Shyna said reading the board.

"Really?" Viren asked. "I am ready. Who is paying?"

"It's a fine board stupid."

"Oh. How much for an intense love making then?"

"Shut up," Shyna chuckled. "Let's go inside the park."

They started walking hand in hand in a breezy atmosphere savoring each other's company.

"What happened shona?" Viren asked her as they walked leisurely in the park. "I am missing my spunky wife today," he said after watching her quiet for long.

"I am worried about Rishabh and Angel. Do you think they should do what they are going to do?"

"I don't know. I am also not sure about their plan but knowing them both, I think they can handle anything."

"Viren," Rishabh's father called him from a distance.

Little surprised, Viren waived at them and went to meet them along with Shyna.

"So Enfield turned to riverfront today. How are you?"

Shyna asked Rishabh's parents.

"We are good. Rishabh is getting married. Her name is Angel. Meet her parents," Rishabh's mom said unable to control her excitement.

Rishabh and Angel's cyclonic pace of executing their plan put Viren and Shyna in a shock. When in shock, you don't move, breathing stops momentarily despite of ample oxygen around, your eyes and mouth compensate by opening more.

"They have gone for a walk to know each other," Rishabh's father said. "By the way he is Viren, Rishabh's publishing agent and his wife Shyna," he introduced them to Angel's parents.

"Publishing agent?" Angel's parents asked with an utter surprise.

"Oh I forgot to tell you. Rishabh is a writer."

"Amazing. I always wanted my son-in-law to be a writer."

Receiving shocks was not Shyna and Viren's style, giving was. So they found it difficult to handle them. The loony couple had impressed each other's parents so much that no one even cared about asking the back ground also, as they generally do in arranged marriages in India. Shyna quickly took Viren aside taking the desperate parent's permission.

"Look at their faces, they are so happy," Shyna said.

"I know and when those two idiots will start their drama, they will be get extremely hurt."

"Shall we tell them everything, so that they can act accordingly and don't get hurt at least?"

Viren contemplated for a while and then said, "Let's go"

"We want to tell you something," Viren said to the parents.

"Oh yes, tell them about your first meeting with Shyna,"

Rishabh's father said. "I still savor that story even after listening it so many times"

"It's about Rishabh and Angel," Shyna said.

With stonewashed smiles, they all looked at the two in anticipation.

"Rishabh and Angel know each other since long. They love each other. They are just playing with you right now," Viren said.

"Impressing you was a part of their plan. It was step one. Now step two is to squabble in front of you and involve you also in the arguments to create tension," Shyna blurted out the plan.

"What's the next step?" Rishabh's mom asked.

"No steps after that, except the final step of marriage," Angel's mom unveiled it before Shyna could, knowing her daughter well.

Viren and Shyna felt a need of someone specialized in a higher medical field who treated patients of having an encounter with crazy families.

"How do you know that?" Shyna asked.

"It must be Angel's plan," Angel's mother said. "Doctors only cut the physical umbilical cord not the emotional one. I have been used to her vivacity but now it's high time she will have to understand a few responsibilities." With joined hands she said to Rishabh's mother, "Please don't mind her craziness, she is very good at heart."

Rishabh's mother held her hands and said, "Please don't get hurt when I say a few bad words to you during the altercation and please bear with my acting, I am not so good at it. Angel is now my daughter too. I would love to be a part of her craziness."

That elated emotion, when you cry and smile at the same time is just one of the many miracles of the God and when you witness it, it seems to be a blessing from almighty. The parents acquiesced to be the part of the plan and act accordingly.

****

"Tom Cruise or Shahrukh Khan?" Rishabh asked for a topic of squabble to Angel. She shook her head.

"Premarital honeymoon"

"No"

"Vasectomy or copper t?"

"Shut up"

"Windows or android?"

"Really?" she chuckled.

"Coconut or Coke?"

"Coconut any day"

"I back that. Parineeti or Priyanka?"

"Rishabh," she wanted him to stop.

"Both are hot mines of talent," but Rishabh was busy working out step two.

"Rishabh," she made him sit on a bench near a bus stand outside the park. Rishabh saw her worried face and sat with opened ears. "They all are extremely happy. We should not do this. I don't want to be a murderer of their smile and excitement. I want to back out of this stupid plan. I am really sorry," she said holding her ears.

Rishabh smiled and hugged her.

"So we are getting hitched today," he said after a prolonged hug.

"Yes," she said elated. "Oh fuck yes, we are getting married," she said giggling.

They sat there looking at the stars, imagining themselves romanticizing everywhere on earth. They were getting high on the feelings when someone interrupted in between.

"You are Angel," a quinquagenarian guy appeared out of nowhere.

"Yes, how do you know me?" Angel asked with a greeting smile, getting up from the bench.

"My daughter was a beggar but now because of you she is in school. Last month she stood first in her class. She always talks about how you would teach them in the park. I am suffering from an incurable disease and I had accepted begging as her fate. That day I watched you both on the traffic signal along with the children with banners. I never thought of taking help from something like NGO and giving her a good life. After your teachings, she used to enlighten me on various aspects of life and how to gain self-respect. I took up a job to earn my bread rather than begging. Thank you is too small a word to express my feelings towards you."

"Its ok uncle," she said. "Those kids deserved a better life."

Though Rishabh was used to get such incessant surprises from strangers greeting and thanking Angel, this time he had tears in his eyes. What he was feeling for her before meeting the old guy intensified after meeting him. For Rishabh breathing had now become synonymous with loving her.

"Please have this sacrament," the old guy gave them a sweet.

Bidding him a bye they sat on the bench again. The stars travelled millions of kilometers and came right in front of their eyes. They felt dizzy at first with head turning heavy. Holding the hands they looked at each other. Slowly their bodies went numb, eyes closing despite of their ardent efforts to keep them open. The last thing they could see was a white van stopping near them.

When Rishabh woke up, the blur view gradually became clear, conscious mind taking over and telling him that the place was familiar. It was the same place where he had found Jaggu soaked in blood. He was tied with a rope on a chair with Angel besides him waking up slowly.

When her conscious mind took over she said, "Bloody motherfucker oldie," in a hoarse voice.

"I know this place," Rishabh said.

"It's your destiny writing place and I am holding the pen," Baba said as he entered the room with four others. The attire of Baba was the same as before but a beard was an add-on this time. "Welcome to my abode. Hope you had a pleasant journey," he said sitting on a chair placed right in front of them.

"Who are you?" Rishabh asked.

"Call me your life wrecker."

"You are Baba," he said recognizing the voice he had heard over the transmitter on Jaggu's jacket. Angel looked at Rishabh and then at Baba, startled with what was happening.

"Yes motherfucker. I am Baba"

"What do you want?"

Baba widened his eyes in state of shock and then started laughing uncontrollably. He fell down from the chair and started rolling on the floor. "What do I want?" he asked, still laughing, gaining stability while getting up.

"I fucking want your life to be ripped off," he shouted

inch closer to their faces, his eyes glaring red and nostrils wide open. "It's because of you," he said pointing a finger at both of them. "You motherfuckers that I had to spend last few days in hiding, like an insect."

Rishabh began his Sherlockism to find ways of safeguarding Angel. Looking at the size of Baba's escorts, fighting was of no use. The only solution was to connect with the outer world and he knew Angel used to keep her cellphone in the back pocket.

"But now elections are over, so Baba is back," he continued with his power laced speech. "You two thought you had a victory. You do not know that you have dug your graves motherfuckers."

Rishabh took out Angel's cell phone slowly from her pocket.

"You ruined my business, I will fucking ruin your lives."

Rishabh dropped the cell phone while typing the message. Baba took the phone and looked at Rishabh with a wicked smile.

"I think you did not hear me dumbass. I said I will ruin your life and no one can prevent that from happening," he threw the cell phone which collided with a wall and a smashed to pieces. "I will take your lives without actually killing you. I will tear you apart without any weapons. I will make your whole life a huge regret. Regret of coming in my way. Neither you will be able to live or die. I will marry Angel."

"Fuck you," Angel snapped wrathfully.

"I like it," Baba said chortling. "You will be good in bed."

Rishabh kicked his balls. Baba went on knees in pain. Escorts treaded heavily towards Rishabh.

"Hold on," Baba said and everyone stopped. "It's ok," he said chuckling. "This pain is nothing compared to what I will give him after marrying his girl and celebrating my honeymoon in his fucking house," he said and started laughing again, going out of control.

"Don't forget to give your best while we decimate you all motherfuckers," Angel said.

Baba gave a sly smile looking straight into Angel's eyes. "Time to unveil my best. Rana, remove the curtain," he said raising his right hand and signaling with his index finger to one of his escorts.

He removed the curtains, behind which was Krishna in a school uniform hanging from a pole unconscious beside a butchered lamb. He had cuts on his face, bruises on his visible knees. He looked weak and haggard. His white shirt and sky blue shorts had blood stains. Malaise travelled down the bodies of Rishabh and Angel when they looked at that gory scene. The unbearable pain resulted in tears in Angel's eyes. She felt broken and devastated. Safety of Krishna was her topmost priority now. She said with a cracking voice, "Please leave Krishna, I will marry you." Rishabh looked at her with tears rolling down his heart. She was his oxygen and Baba was trying to take her away from him. He felt chocked already.

"Look at these two little shits who wanted to decimate me," Baba said and started laughing again. Escorts joined him too. He stood close to Rishabh and Angel without worrying about getting his balls punched again because he was sure that he had debilitated them enough.

"Some mistakes are forgiven, some mistakes are punished but some mistakes are to be reminded for whole life," Baba said standing close to them speaking slowly. "You committed a huge mistake by crusading in my way and I am going to remind you that, every fucking moment of your life. I am not only going to marry her, but I will use her as my sex toy. In fact, I will use her as a prostitute to get my work done from lousy powerful people and you motherfucker," he said to Rishabh, "are going to witness this for your whole life and curse yourself for the mistake you committed." Baba went red with a revenge on his mind. "I am giving you just one night. Go spend a night together and feel the tremendous pain of separation by being together. I will marry her tomorrow morning. It's your responsibility to bring her and please do not try to use your brain otherwise Krishna will look like the other one beside him tomorrow."

Traumatized, Rishabh's eyes only could speak, with tears. From his teary eyes he was watching his life falling apart. The emotions of a broken person are volcanic, they erupt fiercely and burn everything down. The disability of saving Angel from disaster and letting her face it alone devastated Rishabh.

****

"So it's done," Viren said. "You will support their altercation and start squabbling with each other. Dragging them home, you will cancel everything creating total mayhem. Even after their constant persuasion, you will not agree to anything while on the other hand Shyna and I will plan their wedding secretly and surprise them"

"Done," they all placed hands over one another.

"Ok, we shall move now," Shyna said. "They might be coming. If they see us they will smell the plan."

Viren and Shyna left, leaving the desperate parents ready to fight.

"Don't tell anything to our parents," Angel said to Rishabh as they hugged each other after coming out from the van.

They started walking slowly towards the park unable to speak for a while and then Rishabh broke the silence, "You are not going to marry him."

"Krishna is in danger"

"I will save him. Give me some time."

"We only have tonight. If I don't reach to marry him tomorrow morning, he can cause harm to Krishna."

"Just because of this one doubt, you are not going to marry that monster"

"What if the doubt gets real and because of our foolishness a small kid has to bear the consequences? Let me get inside the gang first and save Krishna too. Then I will be your informer and you can easily catch them all with the help of police."

"Are you fucking out of your mind?" Rishabh shouted as the parents watched him speaking loudly in public.

"So what do you want me to do? Be a silent observer to his deviltry," Angel said.

"Look at her, she is shouting at my son just after their first meeting. What will she do after marriage?" Rishabh's mother said stepping into the scene, acting out the plan, along with three others.

"Yes, she is right," Rishabh's father said.

"Your son must have started it. My daughter is a pearl. You will not be able to find a daughter-in-law like her in ages."

"Yes, she is correct," Angel's father said.

The mind of Rishabh and Angel went vacant like an untenanted house. Their face went blank like a new sheet of paper. The epidemic of confusion ripped their brains.

"I do not want stone-hearted pearl. She doesn't even know how to behave in the first meeting with a boy."

"Yah, she is absolutely correct," Rishabh's father corroborated.

"We all saw who shouted first. Your son has no etiquettes of speaking to a lady, MCP."

"True. She is hundred percent correct," Angel's father said.

"Thank God, everything got clear on day one. My son is saved from getting trapped in a cheap family."

"Yah, I was going to say the same thing."

"Do not ever show us your face again. It's all over."

"Yes, it's all over"

"Done, it's all over."

It looked like some negative power was taking revenge from them for spreading so much of positivity. Being helpless is like being paralyzed, it's sickening. Every step away from each other was like a needle piercing in their heart, tearing all the dreams apart, making them numb after a shooting pain. Giving explanation to their parents and clearing the confusion looked frivolous as bigger fear was looming over their heads. It looked like they were destiny's lost kids who did not know how to get back home. Helpless, clueless, directionless, they were dragged out of the park by their parents who gave numerous signals to each other for successfully carrying out their plan but Rishabh and Angel could not notice anything but the fear of their imminent separation.

21

"Thank God it was a fabricated fight. At least our parents are with us. It's only Baba who needs to be taken care of now," Rishabh said to Viren with a glass of whiskey in hand, sitting over a concrete water tank, after Viren cleared everything to him.

"Let's go and break bloody Baba's bum and take Krishna out from there," whiskey spoke through Viren.

"We do not know where his bum is right now"

"We cannot wait till morning Rishabh. Think of something quickly, please."

"Thoughts have ceased to occur in front of that wretched face of Angel. I have never seen her like that. She doesn't deserve to be like that. Her smile can pour life into the dead and today that motherfucker Baba took that away. She was crying, being assaulted in front of me and I was a meek observer. I will not be able to live without her. Please save her Viren, please save her," Rishabh hugged Viren and started crying.

It was going to be the longest and darkest night for them. The irony of the situation was, even the longest night looked very small to find the solution to this grave problem.

****

Baba was as usual in his Pathani kurta when Rishabh brought Angel clad in a red sari in a Shiva temple. The whole temple was covered by Baba's escorts. Rishabh's red eyes and disheveled hair told that he had not slept the whole night. Angel stood there in silence under the head scarf of her sari.

"So the hero brought the bride himself," Baba said smiling ear to ear. "Remove the veil," he said in a stern voice, smile disappeared suddenly.

"What?" Rishabh asked.

"I have seen movies, I don't want to fool myself after marriage. Remove her veil, fast. I don't have enough time."

Rishabh slowly removed the veil with trembling hands. It was Angel.

"She looks stunning, perfectly bangable," Baba said laughing and showing his tobacco stained teeth. Rishabh tightened his fist and clenched his teeth but Angel held his hand and made him calm. She put the veil back on her face.

Baba proceeded to hold the hand of Angel but Rishabh stopped him, "Where is Krishna?" he asked.

"Let me get married first," Baba said, firmly pushing Rishabh aside and taking Angel towards the wedding set up where a pundit was already sitting and ready for chanting mantras.

Baba and Angel sat before the Yajana and the pundit became a parrot chanting the mugged up chants.

Rishabh stood there watching everything with his redshot eyes without a blink, his teeth clenching harder and fist getting tighter. He was not crying, he looked fiercely

173

revengeful. The dribbling anger from his eyes depicted his rage.

"Now you both are husband and wife," pundit concluded after finishing his final chant.

Holding Angel's hand, baba started walking towards Rishabh smiling ebulliently. His revenge was over. He was on the seventh sky.

Reaching close to Rishabh, looking in his eyes directly, he said, "I took your girl and now I will take your money also. Keep watching. You are finished motherfucker, I will take everything you have.

Rishabh stood still without blinking an eye.

"But if you want, I can give you the job of a beggar in my business. See I am not that bad also. I don't know why guys portray me like that.

"Where is Krishna?" Rishabh asked.

Baba started laughing hysterically over his question. Escorts joined him too. After gaining some control he said, "You are a fucking fool. I married your girl and you have not met the kid yet," he started laughing again. "That's the problem with good guys like you, you have a lot of weaknesses," he continued further. "Look at me, look at my freedom and look at you, destitute. You lost your girl and now you will lose the kid too. Tonight I will cut his limbs and make him a beggar again. And not only Krishna, I will make all the kids beggar again."

"I will never be a beggar again," a voice said from behind Baba. He turned to look who it was, only to find Krishna in Jaggu's arms along with inspector Iqbal Sheikh and his police force.

****

Let's take the story a little back where Rishabh and Viren were sitting over a concrete water tank gulping whiskey.

"Please save her Viren, please save her," Rishabh hugged Viren and started crying.

Viren knew if Rishabh broke, everything will go for a toss. He knew he would have to take Rishabh out of his melancholy first, to find the solution to this problem.

"Listen Rishabh," he confronted him. "I want you to focus. We only have one night to save Angel and Krishna. Either you can cry whole night and then for whole life after tomorrow or we can find a way to butt kick that fucking Baba."

Rishabh stopped crying and looked at Viren, "Alright," he said.

"Good. Now focus and try to recall everything in your last encounter with Baba. What was the location, who all were there, how did they look like, what were they doing, everything."

Rishabh's brain started working after Viren fuelled it with a sense of urgency. "The location was in Juhapura, the same where I found Jaggu. Baba was in his black Pathani kurta along with his four escorts. They were well built and stood in four corners."

"You know anybody's name out of those four?"

Rishabh tried to recall the conversation and put some more pressure on his brain to get a clear picture. *"Time to unveil my best. Rana, remove the curtain."*

"Rana, yes, it was Rana, one of the escorts."

"Great"

175

"And I know the person who can take us to him", Rishabh said getting up. "Let's go."

****

"I have his number," Jaggu said at 2am in the morning. "We can trace his location."

"But we need gadgets and support system to handle this operation," Viren said.

"Don't worry, I know where we need to go now," Rishabh said.

****

"Who is it," asked inspector Iqbal Sheikh in a sleepy voice hearing the doorbell. When he opened the door, Rishabh shot instantly, "We need your help."

"It's 2:30 in the morning. My family is sleeping."

"There is a whole police force to take care of your family but a small kid might lose his life despite of us knowing that a help in time could have saved him."

Iqbal looked at three of them and said, "Give me two minutes"

They reached control room. Since Rana already had Jaggu's number and knew him well, he would have sensed the bait so Iqbal told Viren to call him from his own cell phone which was being tapped.

"Hello," Rana said.

"Sir, you must be really tired right now," Viren said.

"Who is it?"

"We have started a midnight body massage at affordable

rates, Sir."

"Who will give the massage?"

"Our trained female professionals from Ukraine Sir. They will loosen you up and relax you like never before."

"Where is the location?"

A technician gave a thumbs up as he deciphered Rana's location. Viren cut the call.

"Where is he?" Iqbal asked the technician.

"Police Commissioner's office"

"What the fuck is he doing there?" Iqbal murmured.

"Come on, let's go," Viren said. "Let's grab the bastard. What are you thinking?"

"Are you stupid? Obviously Krishna is not with him right now. Catching him is of no use. We will have to think of something else."

"But you can take out the information from him after catching him," Jaggu said.

"What if he turns out to be a pachyderm and doesn't tell us anything. Also that might make them aware and then they will keep changing Krishna's location or even worse, they might cause harm to him. We can't take that risk."

"But if we will think so much we will never be able to find Krishna," Viren said.

"He is right," Jaggu said. "Let's catch the bastard. Beat the motherfucker and take out the information."

"Wait a minute," Rishabh interrupted. "Rana will reveal the location himself."

"How?" Viren asked.

"Jaggu, how much do you know Rana? Tell us everything about him, about his weaknesses," Rishabh asked Jaggu.

"Lust is the last name of Rana. Few months back he

bought iPhone 128GB out of which 108 GB is porn. He has a dream of owning a mansion with all female servants serving him nude, inside and outside the house, from driver to gardener to bartenders to everyone. He is a satyromaniac who survives on sex."

"Great," Rishabh said. "Is there anything he hasn't received yet and is longing for?"

"Yes. It's Laila. He keeps nagging her and she keeps ignoring him."

"Where is she right now?"

"It's 3am, she must be at work now."

"Let's go," Rishabh said and they followed him.

Laila was busy with a customer on second floor in room number 8. Rishabh and Jaggu went running towards her while Viren and Iqbal handled Jamnaben.

"Why did you bother Sir," Jamnaben said to Iqbal. "You should have just called me once, I would have rendered my services at your doorstep. And I never knew Jaggu is your friend. He is a loyal customer to us."

"Oh that's okay. I appreciate your warm treatment. I just want to tell you that please start finding another location for your setup. We might get orders to confiscate this place soon."

Jamnaben's lighted up face went dim. "Where will I go Sir? We shifted here sometime back only."

"What are the margins in this business by the way" Viren asked with a curious tone. The other two kept staring at him, flabbergasted.

After settling with customer, Jaggu and Rishabh sat with Laila and explained her the situation.

"You are the one who gave me verbal orgasm that day,

right?" Laila asked Rishabh after listening to them.

"What the fuck. When did you come here?" Jaggu asked Rishabh.

"Before you were dragged and included in Rehmaan Chacha's family and your passion for photography was brought back."

Jaggu went blank for a while and then asked, "You planned everything for transforming me into a better person?"

Rishabh nodded in agreement.

Jaggu jumped over Rishabh and fell on a floor along with him, "Why did you not tell me before fucker?"

"You were in a hospital recovering through photography classes," Rishabh said struggling to get out of his grip.

"And orgasm? How dare you fucking give an orgasm to your would be sister-in-law?"

"Hang on," Laila said. "Did you just proposed me for the marriage?" she asked smiling ear to ear.

They stood up adjacent to each other smiling along with her.

"And what are the overheads in this? How much do you pay to these Jumbos?" Viren asked Jamnaben looking at the guards at the gate.

"Why do you want to enter into the prostitution industry?" Iqbal asked.

"Diversification. It's a highly competitive market these days. You need to diversify to survive."

"But this one is illegal."

"At present, yes. But what if our myopic leaders someday see the revenue of this beautiful service industry and start legalizing things. If saloons are legal, brothels should also be legal. God gave us the need for food, water, oxygen and sex. If restaurants are legal, so should be brothels.

"But most of them are not happy to be a prostitute. They just do it for money."

"I know it's a very low profile job but once it's legalized it can be organized and considered as a respectable profession. By the way, there is a prostitute in every cubicle of a corporate building with a tucked in shirt, a tie and a pair of shiny shoes and they do unthinkable things for money. Look at me, I give blow jobs to get my work done. The whole world is a brothel, why make a fuss about some real pleasurable sex?"

"Okay, let's say it's a good service industry like any other industry but what about the human trafficking generating because of it. How will you justify it?"

"Why do you blame us for that?" Jamnaben retorted this time. "We do our job ethically. It's your job to catch the malpractices. This gentleman is right. Prostitution should be legalized. In medical field they trade human organs. Why haven't you banned the medical field yet?"

Meanwhile Laila and Jaggu could not control to express their feelings for each other. "If you are done with your post proposal moments, can we please call Rana now?" Rishabh said to the amorous couple who were getting intimate in front of him.

"That way we will have to ban everything. But what's your problem? What you are complaining for?" Iqbal said. "You have an inspector sitting in front of you allowing you to run a brothel, informing you about the raids well in advance, what else do you want? In our country you cannot do certain things openly so they are labelled as illegal with a provision of parallel system for running it smoothly."

"If paid sex is so illegal what you have to say about dowry. It is also illegal by the law but people take it openly," Viren said. "I really don't understand the logic behind dowry."

"I am sorry that you have to do this because of me," Jaggu said to Laila.

"It's ok, we are doing this for Krishna. After this, we will start afresh."

"Your post-marriage holiday is on me," Rishabh said.

Laila picked up her phone and called Rana.

"Hello Rana," Laila said on the phone.

"Your fingers must have worked really hard to dial my number. Shall I come over there to give you a massage, just a manicure I mean?" Rana said in his lusty voice.

"I need you Rana. All men are dogs, except you. I am sorry that it took me so long to understand you, but now I know, that you are the only person who truly cares about me. Please come over Rana, I need you, badly," Laila said with an intense sorrow in her voice.

Rana had Bajaj Pulsar 220cc bike which transformed into a jet aircraft. In no time, he reached that under construction building where Laila was waiting for him along with Rishabh and Jaggu who were in the adjacent room by now. Like a cartoon from a road runner show he ran on the second floor leaving Viren, Iqbal and Jamnaben jaw dropped.

His chest hair got curls with vibrations produced by his thumping heart under the heavy muscles resulted from a non-vegetarian protein diet. Shutting the door, he stood there in shock catching his breath, Laila in front of him in a seductive skimpy clothes.

"I missed you Rana," Laila said with a seductive voice.

Rana was bankrupt of words, with Laila in front of him in a closed room. He kept staring at her with ballooned eyeballs trying to believe his luck.

"Come here Rana, come into my arms. Take me to another world. This one is full of betrayers. I can only trust you now, Rana."

He ran towards her and started kissing her with full force. Carrying her onto the bed, he started removing his shirt.

"Hold on Rana," Laila said. "I want you to go slow. I am all yours and tonight is not time bound. We have a lot of time. Please sit beside me."

Those were the hypnotic words by Laila thrown on Rana and they worked like a best sedative drug. He sat beside her and kept looking at his fantasy sitting in the revealing clothes.

"You know when I was small I used to sit with my brother like this and look at the stars."

That *brother* word was an emergency stop on the heavy pumping of blood in Rana's body. Everything restored to normal. He sat straight.

Today I miss him a lot. He was my shield, my protector and after a long time, I have found the same quality in someone. It's you Rana, it's you," she said taking deep breath. "Please don't leave me Rana. I don't have enough energy left now to go through the pain of getting hurt again." Tears came out of her eyes.

"What happened Laila?" her tears credited few words in Rana's empty verbal account that night.

"Nothing. I don't want to recall anything. Tell me about yourself. What are you doing these days?" Laila prepared the trap after placing the bait.

"Some usual stuff from Baba. Payment collection and hiding a small kid."

"Since when did you start kidnapping?"

"Oh no, it's not like that. That idiot wants to marry a girl and kid is just a mode to get her. I always believed that he is some sort of stupid. Bloody idiot should just abduct the girl and marry her, why so much of drama? He said he wants the girl and her boyfriend to go through a lot of pain. Motherfucker has put us in the pain. Now we have to look after the kid for the whole night ruining our sleep"

"Poor kid," she sighed. "Has he eaten something?"

"I don't know? There is another other guy with him to take care of that."

"Don't be a monster, Rana. Just ask him about the kid right away. Show some kindness also at times."

"Alright, alright. Calm down my lady."

He picked up his phone to dial but could not connect.

"What happened to this stupid device? I am not able to connect to anyone."

Laila pressed the cell phone signal jammer surreptitiously which was placed beneath the bed.

"Here, take my phone," she gave him Viren's phone.

Rana took the phone and she released the jammer, clearing the signal. Rishabh gave her the gadget before departing from the room. Since technician had older technology, he had to attach a small chip in Viren's cell phone in order to trace the call. He could not directly trace Rana's phone.

Within seconds, after Rana connected the call to his accomplice, technician alerted Iqbal who along with his team immediately went to the location of hiding.

Jaggu broke the door with a single kick.

"Jaggu?" Rana asked in utter surprise.

"Nah, your father who is going to whip your ass."

Rishabh took Laila outside the room while the two six-plus feet frames were tearing the room apart. The ripples in the air post their collision could be felt in the building. The bloody fight ceased when Iqbal's men took control and arrested Rana.

****

"The problem with the bad guys is that they misconstrue the strength of the good guys as their weakness," Rishabh replied to Baba who was cold by now looking at the police force and Krishna. "Your reason to fight was revenge while mine was my life. You were bound to lose with a smaller reason."

Once the tornedo was settled in Baba's mind and he got his senses back, he looked here and there in desperation for help. When his eyes fell on Angel, he erupted laughing uncontrollably.

"You turned out to be an intelligent fool. You worked so hard in getting Krishna but ended up giving your girlfriend to me," Baba said. "Now you listen to me and listen me well," Baba said with a faded smile and grave voice. "You girlfriend is now my wife legally and you look like an educated person to me so by law, I am now legally permitted to do all sorts of sexual activities with my wife. So before I begin my honeymoon right here in front of everyone, take your khaki puppies back."

"Happy honeymoon motherfucker," another voice came

behind Baba and this time it was Angel in a light blue top and dark blue denims.

Rishabh smiled and hugged her tightly. They hugged as if they will never let the bad happen ever again. They were just not able to leave each other after fighting a tornado last night.

Baba's confusion expanded like universe. "Who the hell did I get married to then?" Baba asked finally with a shaking voice.

The lady in a sari took out the veil and it was Angel again, but then she started removing something from her face very slowly. Once the mask came out, Sandy appeared with a smiling face.

"Come on Baba. Let's go for our honeymoon," he said.

****

Let's take the story again a little back where Rishabh and Viren were sitting over a concrete water tank gulping whiskey.

"And I know the person who can take us to Rana," Rishabh said.

"Perfect. Who is it?'

"Jaggu"

"Let's go then"

"Wait. We need a spurious Angel also, in case we get late in finding Krishna. I can't let Angel be present even near to that monster."

"Shyna can do it. She knows a person who can make a mask of any person on the planet but that guy stays in Mumbai."

"You know how to arrange a private chartered plane, right?"

"Right," Viren smiled.

With Shyna's hard work and Sandy's grace, Baba was left clueless about his imminent public ridicule.

"You all will die motherfuckers, you all will die. This police is my puppet. Going to jail is like a weekend party for me. Before I am back, do your loved ones a favor. Book yourself a place in a crematorium motherfuckers."

"You won't be back for a very long time Baba," another voice came from behind Baba.

It was Police Commissioner, Mr. Vijaykant Rathore. Iqbal stood in the alert position, "Sir, you?" he asked.

"Good job Iqbal. I like your dedication. They told me you were on the operation for the whole night."

"Hey Commissioner," Baba roared. "Don't forget your Godfather is still alive. He will transfer you in some remote village where they will rape your wife and daughter every day to keep your mouth shut."

"The godfather you are talking about is out of power. His arrest warrant is generated against the molestation of a journalist and we have received fresh orders to immediately clean the filth. Iqbal," he said, "arrest the bastard and show him what pain in the ass is? I will personally visit and treat him in the third degree."

Iqbal and team arrested everyone. "I will not leave you motherfuckers," Baba kept repeating that while he was being taken away by the police.

22

"Are you cold?" he asked after leaving Baba da dhaba.

"Fucking freezing," she replied.

"Then use your heater."

"Alright," she said and Rishabh felt her hands on his groin.

But a chilly winter's incessant hugs and kisses failed human heaters.

"We will pass through a market in some time. Let's buy the jackets," Rishabh said.

"How about stealing?" suggested the crazy girl.

The bike stopped outside a shop named '*Daddu k garam kapde*'.

Rishabh went inside the shop and came running outside after few minutes with bags. Angel was ready with the bike. She raised the accelerator as soon as Rishabh jumped on the bike. Two people ran after them but the swift R1 was lost in no time.

He made her wear a jacket and a track over her shorts on a running bike. He wore one too and a beautiful couple in black jackets on black R1 dived into the ocean of blissfulness.

It was 11pm and the roads were empty in the chilly weather. While driving, Angel saw some people sleeping on a footpath. She slowed down the bike. Everyone had a quilt but one lady and her son had just a bed sheet and they were shivering in cold. Daddu ke garam jackets were put on their withered shivering bodies but they were still cold and hungry too.

Rishabh gave them the cookies from *Baba da Dhaba* which they finished without leaving a mark.

"It's so chilling today," the small kid said.

"Thank God you came otherwise we would have passed away till the morning," mother said.

"But mother I can't sleep in this bed sheet. I need a quilt like Rani," kid said looking at the row of people under quilts beside him. "Her father brought it for her. Where is my father?"

"I am really sorry son. I will bring a quilt for you tomorrow from anywhere," mother said with moist eyes and heavy heart. "Just sleep for tonight inside this bed sheet. Tomorrow you will definitely sleep inside the quilt."

"But mother I can't sleep. It's freezing so much tonight."

"Ok listen, I have an idea," Rishabh said. All three looked at him in anticipation.

Moments later Rishabh and Angel were inside the bed sheet smiling and looking into each other's eyes lying side by side. Kid slept peacefully inside the same bed sheet hugging Rishabh from behind and wearing Angel's jacket. Mother wore Rishabh's jacket and hugged Angel.

"You have got beautiful eyes," Angel said.

"Yes, because they watch you all the time."

ABOUT THE AUTHOR

Jaikishan Hirani, a pantheist and an Instrumentation and Control engineer is an Amdavadi, who always takes help of a pen and a paper in trying to make this complicated life simpler. Crazigasm is his second book after his debut novel Corruption in Construction. Born and brought up in a joint family, he cherishes the family talks and warm relationships over dinner. A movies and TV series enthusiast and a nocturnal writer, he loves to spend time with his wife and nature together. He can be contacted at Jaikishan.hirani@gmail.com